Under Open Skies

Super Cowboy Rides

Advanced Praise
for **SUPER COWBOY RIDES**

"The little boy, Tommy, reminds me of Calvin from the **Calvin and Hobbes** comic strip by Bill Watterson because of his mischievousness. It is such a fun book to read!" -- **Celese Sanders** (syndicated columnist of "Little Bits Of Life")

"**Super Cowboy Rides** reminds me of when I was a boy and we would visit my grandparents' farm in Utah where my cousins would try, in a loving way, to kill me. It has a ring of authenticity that could only be accomplished by growing up on a farm or ranch. I loved each chapter, but once I reached the end of the book I realized I had been taught some important lessons. This is a book that boys will love as well as girls who look for the good in everyone." -- **Jack Weyland** (Author of "Charlie" and other Y.A. novels.)

"This is the perfect family trip 'read out loud' book. You are on the edge of your seat the entire time wondering what this little cowboy will do next! We laughed so hard, and my 8-year-old kept begging me to not stop reading. This book reels you in from the first page. We will be adding this fantastic book to our home library." -- **Stephanie Ashcraft** (New York Times best-selling author)

In a style reminiscent of early Richard Peck, Daris Howard introduces us to Tommy Johnson, super cowboy and super storyteller. The reader is invited to share in the many first-hand adventures of a five to six-year-old boy raised on a dairy farm in southeast Idaho during the economically hard 1960s. But our guide has everything any super cowboy could want: parent to love and guide him and brothers to help him get into and out of trouble.

Tommy's best trait is that he gives every project his best effort and many times his heart. He catches untamed cats to helping his brother try out a new parachute design from the barn loft; he drags a reluctant bum lamb home from a generous neighbor and turns it into a best friend despite many unplanned for bruises; and he morns a dear neighbor's sudden death. He continuously touches our funny bones, and our hearts, as well as our memories of the innocence and insight of youth. -- **Julie Clark** (Children's Literature Professor at BYU Idaho)

"Super Cowboy Rides" is a touching and well-written story that will cheer your day. Young readers will discover the past, and older readers reminisce amid tears and laughter as they follow the adventures of Tommy and Tippy. -- **Anne Bradshaw** (Author of "Dingo" (a teenage mystery) and other books.)

"God Bless Daris Howard! He's conjured up a world that's almost gone now, in these evocative tales of boyhood, back-in-the-day, in rural America. His stories, rich with honest sentiment, ring true. He not only remembers well what life was like in a simpler time, he shares it all with ease, and a fine eye for detail.

Now times may change, but human nature doesn't change. And his young hero is learning lessons in life... I appreciate the warmth, the wit, and the solid values found in these nostalgic vignettes of American life." -- **Chip Deffaa** (Author of *Voices of the Jazz Age* (University of Illinois Press) and a dozen other published books and plays.)

What makes Daris' stories so engaging is we can see something of ourselves in Super Cowboy. Anyone who has grown up on a farm in a rural setting has taken part in at least some of his adventures, but the events that surround little Tommy transcend the setting. Who hasn't loved a pet, felt inadequate at school, or wondered where babies come from? I love the twists at the ends of the stories. "Sunday School" and "The Witch's House" will always be my favorites. Entertaining, poignant – it's a great book when we can laugh and cry and feel the better for it. -- **Judy Dewey** (Director Madison Library District - Rexburg, Idaho)

From a 2nd grade teacher and her students:

"Teachers are always looking for a realistic way to teach children about bullying. This is a great resource and a great story. This was such a fun book." -- **Peggy Hawkins, Teacher, Lincoln Elementary**

"It was the best book I ever read. It was funny too." -- **Kai**

"I liked it because it showed a hard life and because it was hilarious. I love Super Cowboy Rides." -- **Elliana**

"Super Cowboy Rides was the best book I have ever heard. Super Cowboy Rides is an awesome book." -- Kim

Under Open Skies

Super Cowboy Rides

by
Daris Howard

Publishing Inspiration - St. Anthony, Idaho

Publishing Inspiration
St. Anthony, Idaho
Copyright © 2011 by Daris Howard

This book is a work of fiction. Names, characters, places, organizations,
and incidents either are products of the author's imagination or are used
fictitiously. Any resemblance to actual persons, living or dead, events or
organizations is entirely coincidental.

Cover art by Mark McKenna

ISBN-10: 1629860026
ISBN-13: 978-1629860022

Manufactured in the United States Of America

www.publishinginspiration.com

Dedication

I dedicate this book to my wife and children. I started writing stories for them, and this book is part of the result of that effort. In particular, I dedicate it to my oldest daughter, Celese. She is the first of my children that I started writing stories for.

TABLE OF CONTENTS

1

A Pup Named Tippy

Cats are dumb animals. The tame ones are, anyway. Most of the cats around our farm are wild, but my sisters dress up the few that aren't in little doll clothes, put them in wicker baskets, and take them for walks like they are babies. The cats put up with this, and that's why I know they are dumb animals. You wouldn't find a dog putting up with that. Dogs are much smarter than cats.

I wanted a dog for as long as I can remember, which must be close to an eternity. I don't know how long an eternity is, but I figure it must be about six years, since that is how old I am. Okay, so I'm not six yet, but I will be come summer. That's old enough to have a dog. I begged and pleaded with my Dad for a dog.

"Why don't you go play with the cats?" he asked.

That's when I had to tell him that I think cats are dumb animals. Besides, have you ever heard of a cat coming when you whistle or running with you to chase butterflies? Have you ever heard of a cat going hunting with you or stalking game? I'm sure you haven't, and neither have I, except for an occasional mouse, and what kind of an adventure is that? A five-year-old boy needs adventure, and a cat, well, that is just ludicrous. I'm not quite sure what that word means, but Mom always says it when she wants to tell someone how silly something is.

Anyway, I needed some adventure. When our television worked, I would watch astronauts preparing to go to the moon. President Kennedy said we wanted to get there before the Russians. I think the Russians are from Mars or something.

I saw a movie about people from Mars coming to earth and they weren't very nice. I'm sure that is why President Kennedy doesn't want them on the moon.

Someday I will be an astronaut. I asked my Dad if there were astronauts where we live. He said the astronauts lived in Florida, and that it is a long way from Idaho. So I suppose I will have to wait until I am older.

I thought I could be a cowboy. Dad had been a cowboy when he was younger, and we watched John Wayne on the television sometimes. But a cowboy has to have guns, and my mom won't even let me have toy ones. When I pretend to be a cowboy, I have to use a stick for my gun. There's not much adventure in that.

That only leaves a dog. A boy can have a lot of adventure with a dog. But I had asked my dad for a dog a billion times, give or take a few, and I had never gotten anywhere. I figured my dad never had a dog, and so he didn't know how important they are. Then one day, as I was looking at some old pictures, I came across one of a boy standing beside the biggest dog I had ever seen. The dog stood nearly as tall as the boy. Next to them was a huge sled on metal runners.

"Who is that dog?" I asked.

"That dog," my dad said, "was named Bud. He was a Great Dane."

"What made him so great?"

My dad smiled. "That's just the type of dog he was."

"Who is the boy?"

"The boy is me," my dad answered, beaming with the pride that comes from owning a fine animal.

I began to get excited. My dad had a mysterious past that I didn't know about. "You had a dog?"

My dad got a strange look in his eye as he answered. "When I was just a boy, one of my assignments was to go down the road to the neighbor's house and exchange eggs for milk. In the winter I would hitch Bud to the sleigh, and he would pull me down and back. In the summer, I had a big wagon I used. One day, a rabbit crossed our path on the way to get milk, and Bud chased it, pulling me through ditches and into trees. I was hurt, and the wagon was broken. After that, my father got rid of Bud."

As my dad told it, I could tell it had been a hard moment for him, and that it probably wasn't a good time to ask for a dog again. In fact, I wondered if I could ever ask for a dog again.

However, a few days later, my dad came home and announced that the whole family was going for a drive. "Where are we going?" everyone asked excitedly.

"Crazy!" my dad replied. "We're all just going crazy!" That is Dad's way of telling us not to ask any more questions.

We all pushed and shoved our way into our old station wagon. There were eight of us kids. John was oldest at 17 with a year and a half to two years between each of us, except me and Willie. Willie, who was two, was three years younger than me. John and Jason were both in high school. Daniel was in eighth grade, Mary was in sixth, Josie was in fourth, and Albert was in second.

Once we were all in, we started rolling slowly along. Soon we reached the river and traveled the road that rambled along it. I was one of the youngest in the family, and since the car didn't have enough seats, I had to sit on someone's lap. I hate sitting on another person's lap, except that I can sit by a window, and I do like that. I mostly like watching the river, because there are so many interesting things to see, especially in the spring.

With the window slightly down I could hear the birds singing. It was still early March, so chunks of ice were floating down the river, but the sun was shining, and they would soon be melted. Although the ground was mostly white as far as I could see, patches of brown dirt showed through here and there on the south side of the trees and buildings where the sun was warmest.

Every once in a while, I could hear the honking of geese winging their way back from the south, and I even saw a swan. They are so pretty as they mark out their territory and defend it from intruders.

On one stretch of the river, I could see a beaver dam under construction. I hoped to catch a glimpse of the beaver that was building it, but that never happened. The farmers often cuss the beavers because they fill irrigation canals with dams that block the water flow. But I think they are interesting animals, not because I have seen that many, but because I can't seem to build a dam that will hold water, even in our small irrigation ditches.

I took a deep breath of the fresh air coming in the window. It was still cold from the lingering ice and snow, and yet the warm, thawing wind blowing from the south brought a smell that said summer was coming.

We crossed the rusty, one-way bridge, and drove along until we came to the old Silverstein place. They had a nice, cozy little home. That's what my dad called it. My mom called it rundown.

The Silversteins were an older couple that had worked hard all of their lives. Old Mr. Silverstein had large, rough hands from years of hard farm work. His skin was leathery from many hours outdoors, even in the winter. Old Mrs.

Silverstein had skin about as soft as a saddle left in the rain, and more wrinkled than a flour sack stuffed in a grain bin for a winter.

Dad always said that even if their home wasn't fancy, "a person could feel comfortable there coming in from the cold and putting his feet up."

Home cooking, with smells of bacon, steak, eggs, potatoes, fresh garden vegetables, and homemade bread, hung in the air and drifted in the car window as we pulled into the driveway.

Mr. Silverstein stepped out onto the porch, and my dad went to shake his hand.

"Here to see what we talked about," my dad said.

"They're out in the barn," Mr. Silverstein replied.

By this time, the seven of us children had climbed out of the old red rambler and were following them to the barn. I had to trot to keep up. My mother would usually stay in the car with my two-year-old brother, Willie, but this time she bundled him up and brought him along. When we reached the barn, Mr. Silverstein swung the door wide. As it groaned to a stop, he pointed to a horse stall. "They're in there. You're welcome to help yourself."

A dog poked her head around the corner, and as she did, I heard the whimpering of puppies. I shot over to the stall in an instant. The mother dog rushed back to her pups, leery of her new visitors. As I looked at the little bundles of fur, they padded here and there and came right up to me.

"Well, which one would you like, Tommy?" my father asked me.

"What made you change your mind about getting a dog?" my mother asked my father.

"They're free," he replied.

"We better get a male," my mother said. "We don't want puppies."

One pup caught my eye. As the other dogs ran around and played, he tried to chase them, but tripped all over himself. He was twice the size of the others, and his paws were about the size of my hand. I reached out to him and clicked my tongue, and he wagged his way toward me. Just before he got to me, he tripped and tumbled end over end, almost rolling into my lap. Everyone laughed.

"I think that one has a different father than the rest," Mr. Silverstein said. "I tend to think the father of the others was Olsen's Blue Heeler, but I think this one is out of Judson's Great Dane."

"I vote for this one," I said, knowing I didn't have much say. We would get whatever my father and mother decided.

"Look at the paws on him," Daniel said. "He's going to grow up to be a horse."

Daniel was third oldest and joked a lot.

"I'm sure it would cost a fortune to feed him," my mother added, agreeing with Daniel.

However, at the mention of a Great Dane, I had seen that look come over my dad's face.

"Oh, it won't be that bad," he said. "We always have some old milk at the barn, and he can eat a few table scraps now and then."

"With the size of him, maybe we could just tie him to the manger and feed him hay," John, my oldest brother, suggested.

"And saddle and ride him," Daniel added.

My dad picked the puppy up and looked at it. "Sure enough, it's a male," he announced.

I'm not sure how a person tells those kind of things. I think it is written on the underside somewhere, kind of like all of my toy cars that Albert tells me say "Made in Taiwan" underneath. I picked the dog up to look to see where the writing was, but I didn't see any. Everyone laughed at me for trying. I'm sure it was because they knew I can't read. But it didn't matter. I had a dog.

Mr. Silverstein rounded us up a box to put the pup in. I got to hold it on my lap all the way home. As we drove, we had to decide on a name.

"How about Rufus?" Mary, my oldest sister, suggested. "Rufus is a good dog's name."

"That would be good," Daniel chimed in. "That way we could call him Doofus for short."

I couldn't see how Doofus was short for Rufus, but I didn't like the idea of naming my dog that. "I don't like Rufus," I complained.

"Look at his four white paws," Josie, my second sister, said. "Maybe we could call him Mitsy, since he's all brown, except for his four white mitts."

I shook my head. "Mitsy is a girl's name."

"We could name him Paw, for his four white paws," Daniel said.

My father frowned. "Pa? Excuse me!"

"Well, then, how about paw, paw, paw, paw?" John asked.

"We could yell, 'Here Paw Paw' to call him," Daniel said.

"I don't think so," my dad countered.

"Oh, look," Mary said. "His paws aren't all that's white. He has a white tip on the end of his tail."

"You sure that's fur and not white dog doo?" Daniel asked.

"Dog doo would be brown," John answered.

"How about Tippy?" Mary suggested.

"That would work," Daniel said. "Then we could call him Dippy for short."

I couldn't see how Dippy was short for Tippy, but this time I was overruled, and Tippy it was. Just as we were getting home, I felt something warm run down my leg. I let out a gasp, and those closest to me looked.

"Tippy is wet," Daniel said, holding his nose. "I'm glad you're holding the dog and I'm not."

John didn't seem to think it was all that funny, as it was his lap I was sitting on, and he was afraid it would soak into his pants, too.

"It looks like the tip of his tail is now yellow," Daniel teased.

When we reached home, John nearly dumped me out the door, and I barely kept the box with Tippy upright. Everyone bailed out fast because the smell was enough to make our eyes water. As for myself, I was so glad to have a dog that I didn't even care that he had wet on me. Well, okay, so I cared, but I was still glad to have a dog.

Mom looked at me. "Let's get you in and get you cleaned up. The older boys can fix him a bed in the barn."

I didn't want my brothers to be the ones to fix the bed. I wanted to do it. But I knew better than to argue. I rushed into the house to change. Unfortunately, I only have two sets of work clothes, and the others were in the wash. That was not about to stop me. I dug them out of the dirty clothes hamper, switched into them, and tore out to the barn, arriving before my brothers even got the box there.

In one part of the barn, where our calves are, we have little stalls for each individual calf. We made Tippy a bed in one of those. He was only a bit smaller than a baby calf anyway, so he fit right in.

I got a bowl and put some milk in it. Tippy was hungry, but he didn't seem to know what to do. He had probably only nursed. Daniel took Tippy's head and dipped his nose into the milk. Tippy licked his nose and decided it was pretty good. He tried to drink, but he couldn't seem to figure out how to lap like a normal dog. He would put his lower jaw down into the bowl and let the milk run into his mouth, and then he would gulp it down. He couldn't get the lowest part of the milk that way, so he would tilt his head, but he kept spilling the milk. We soon realized we needed a bigger bowl, because even though he was a puppy, he drank nearly a gallon of milk for each meal.

While my brothers went off to milk the cows, I sat there with Tippy and talked to him while he ate. Someone brought him out a few scraps of food from the house, and he ate that, too. Pretty soon he was so full he couldn't move. He looked like a milk can on sticks. In fact, he ate so much he got a stomach ache.

"It looks like he's foundered," Daniel said, looking at Tippy, who laid there groaning while I stroked his head. But in an hour, Tippy was back up and ready to play.

As Tippy grew over the next few weeks, he seemed somewhat confused. He apparently thought he was a calf, since he was raised with the calves. But I think he thought he was a special calf because I would take him places with me.

When we let the calves out into a pen to romp, they would bunt each other. Tippy tried to bunt heads with a calf, but when their heads hit, Tippy toppled end over end. He was daffy for at least a day. Dogs don't have thick, skull-butting kinds of heads.

It wasn't long before something else happened, and we realized we had to move him. One of our old cows had slipped in the barn, and was having trouble walking. My dad decided we would use her for a nurse cow. We would get her into a pen every day when it was time to milk, and turn some calves in on her.

Tippy thought he was a calf, so it was only natural that one day he decided it was his turn to nurse. He worked his way through into the pen and got into position. The cow wasn't paying any attention, as she was chewing the grain we had given her, but when Tippy latched on, she knew immediately that something was wrong.

Calves only have bottom teeth in the front of their mouths when they are born. I know this because, after they are fed, I like to hold out my hand and let the calves suck on it. It's a gooey, tickley feeling. However, Tippy, being a dog, had both top and bottom teeth, and when he latched on, he really latched. The cow, like my dad would say, wound up like a soccer player, with the intent of kicking Tippy into the middle of the next week. When she released, she hit him square in the backside.

Tippy had a good hold, though, and he flipped upside down as he flew through the air with his teeth still clenched shut. The cow's udder stretched out like a giant rubber band, and then, with a sudden pop, Tippy snapped off and slammed into the wall.

The cow spun around to face him, eyes on fire, knocking calves all over the place, as she did a buckin' bronco hop and kick. I could see that she planned to kill Tippy, and, with one quick jump, I was in the pen with a stick to turn the cow back around. No cow was going to mess with my dog!

Tippy just lay on the ground, the breath knocked out of him. I gathered him in my arms and dragged him out of the pen, since he was too big for me to carry. The cow eyed us suspiciously.

Tippy hasn't tried to sneak a free snack from any cow since then. He is pretty lazy anyway, so he is happy to just let someone bring his food to him.

2

Doing the Lamba Walk

Spring is my favorite time of year. The trees leaf out, and the air becomes warmer. After a long winter everything seems fresh and new. And most important, I get to play outside.

In the spring, the snow melts, leaving lots of clean mud to play in. My mother told me that "clean mud" is an oxymoron. I don't know what an oxymoron is. I think it must mean fun.

The smell of sagebrush on the north desert is strongest in the springtime. I love that smell. I learned that when I can also smell wild onions, it is lambing season.

There is a sheep ranch not too far down the road. When it is time for the baby lambs to be born, they cover long rows of lambing sheds with tarps that I can see flapping in the wind. They keep lights on all night, and I can hear sheep bleating clear over to our house.

When Mom isn't looking, I sneak away down the road to the lambing sheds. Old Mr. Brown gives me jobs to help out. Unfortunately, it is usually cleaning out one of the stinkin' sheep pens.

"You might as well make yourself useful so you're not underfoot," he says, handing me a pitchfork.

I love to wander down the aisles and stop at the pens with the newborn lambs. If I stay there too long, the mother sheep stamps her foot and baas to warn me not to get any closer.

Some are more temperamental than others. Sometimes I climb up on the fence to get a closer look at the nursing lambs. As they drink, their little tails wag, like they are caught in the feather picker.

I had only had Tippy about a month when I heard the baaing of sheep.

Before I went to bed that night, I looked down the road, and sure enough, the lights were shining brightly. The next morning, as soon as we finished chores, I was on my way.

When I got there, I wandered among the sheep pens, looking at the newborn lambs. I stopped at one and climbed up on the fence as I always did, but this particular ewe didn't like it. She rammed the fence, which caused me to lose my balance and flop on my back in the aisle. When I looked up, there was Old Mr. Brown.

Mr. Brown was what my dad called a "salty sheepman." He uses more interesting words than anyone I know. One day, last year, I had gone to visit the sheep camp with Albert, who is just older than me. When we came home, I used some of the words I heard Mr. Brown say. My mother's face turned red, and she washed my mouth out with soap.

"She's a darned old bossy thing, isn't she?" Mr. Brown said, as he pulled me to my feet. "She's a might bit protective. She could take on a wolf pack and kick their furry butts to the Arctic. She's a dang good sheep, though; always gives me at least two lambs."

Suddenly, his eyes sparkled as he continued. "This year, however, she gave me three. She shoved the runt away. Usually they would die, but I'll be darned if he's not just like his mother. Come see what I mean."

He took me to the outside pen, where the older lambs and the ewes were in one large group. Here the little lambs would frisk about and butt each other.

"There he is," Old Mr. Brown said. "There's the little fur-ball."

He pointed to a lamb that was much smaller than the rest. The little lamb snuck up on a ewe that was nursing her own lambs. He got up near her back end, and then got under a lamb twice his size. He knocked the bigger lamb off of the teat, taking the milk for himself. The little lamb only got a few good gulps before the ewe felt udder distress as the two lambs fought for position.

Mr. Brown continued to explain the situation. "Sheep have an inborn survival mentality to protect their own. A sheep may reject one of their lambs to guarantee the survival of the others. That's why his mother shoved him away."

When the ewe noticed the imposter, she turned to chase after him, tromping her own lambs in the process. The little lamb bounded away, the ewe right on his tail.

Around the pen they went, with all of the other sheep joining in the chase.

"Won't he get hurt?" I asked.

"Nah," Mr. Brown said, "you just keep a-watchin'."

The little lamb darted through a hole in the fence. Some of the bigger sheep crashed into the fence, but a couple of little lambs followed him through.

"Can't keep that little burr-magnet in the pen for nothin'," Old Mr. Brown said. "When his mother didn't want him, I put him in the bum lamb pen, but he was out in two shakes of a lamb's tail. Found his way out here before we could find a surrogate mother for him."

The sheepmen call the lambs that are rejected or orphaned "bum lambs." I had watched the men try to get a ewe that had lost her lambs to feed an orphaned one by skinning out the ewe's dead lamb and putting the skin on the bum lamb. If the men are lucky, the ewe will smell her lamb's skin and think it is her own until she has accepted the new one. Then the dead lamb's skin can be removed.

There are usually more bum lambs than ewes to feed them, so many die. Sometimes the sheepmen try to bottle feed those they can. Once in a while, Old Mr. Brown lets me do that, which is a lot better than cleaning out stinkin' sheep pens.

"Yip," Old Mr. Brown continued. "This little bummer decided we weren't getting to him fast enough, so he took matters into his own hooves." He chuckled at his own joke, then went on. "He just broke out of the bum lamb pen, though I can't figure how, and he came out here to fend for himself."

I watched as the other little lambs that got out went crazy, racing around the pen, crying to get back in. Their mothers stood on the other side, frantically bleating to them. Meanwhile, the little bum lamb waited until everything had cleared, then went back in through the same hole and started looking for another ewe to steal a meal from.

Mr. Brown caught the other two lambs and put them over the fence to their mothers. "It doesn't matter how often I fix the holes in the fence; he finds another one. Not only that, but he leads these other rejects of nature out, and they can't find their way back in."

"Anyway," he continued, "I was thinking that he would be the perfect lamb for a little boy. I was thinking you might be just the one for him."

I couldn't believe it. My own lamb!

"Of course," he continued, "you would have to catch him. Me and my men just don't have time to help you."

I assured him that I would catch him, and that I would take good care of him.

"Well, then," he said, "Get him caught and get him home before your mother calls wondering where you are."

He didn't have to tell me twice. I was about ready to scramble over the fence when he put his hand on my shoulder.

"You don't want to go doing that. Some old sheep would tromp you into compost. Just wait 'til he comes out, then we'll close up the hole, and you can catch him."

It wasn't long until I had my chance. The little bum lamb had found an unsuspecting ewe and was feeding. Soon the chase was on, and the little lamb ran out of the pen to safety.

Old Mr. Brown blocked the hole and put the stragglers back in. "Now's your chance," he said. "You better keep him going, or he'll find another way in."

I took off after the lamb as fast as I could go, but the gap between us widened. Here I was five years old, and a two-week-old lamb could outrun me. Around and around we went, past the storage building and past the ram pen. The hired hands cheered us on. Old Mr. Brown's line about them being too busy to help me catch the lamb was a bunch of bull. They sure had plenty of time to watch.

I realized that I was making no headway playing ring-around-the-sheep-pen. I decided to cut him off at the pass. As he headed around the storage shed again, I darted around the other side. When he saw me, he nearly rammed into me trying to stop. I jumped for him and missed, landing in a pile of manure.

As I lay there, Old Mr. Brown said, "Hurry, boy, he's heading for the sheep pen!"

I jumped to my feet and turned to cut him off before he got there, afraid he would find some hole in. We reached the pen at the same time, and the race continued. As we headed around for about the fifth time, I caught sight of the docking pen and had an idea.

Because these pens are for catching lambs, they need to be built tighter, with gates that can be shut to enclose smaller areas. I would try to head him in there.

I ran around the lambing shed to head him off. I got in position to turn him toward the docking pen, running to block his way.

The men cheered me in my efforts, yelling, "Smart move!" and "You've got him now!" Somehow I chased him in there and was able to close the gate.

One of the men gave me a piece of twine from a straw bale, and I climbed over the fence. The lamb was running at full speed around the pen, bleating in panic. I cornered him and walked toward him, gently calling, "Here lamby, lamby." He lowered his head and charged straight for me, hitting me in the stomach with all ten pounds of fury.

Down I went, gasping for breath. I heard Old Mr. Brown say, "He's sure a spunky little feller." I didn't know if he meant me or the lamb, but I began to question if I really wanted this lamb.

"Show him who's boss!" the men yelled, and, "Get up and teach him a lesson!"

I hauled myself to my feet and drew closer to the lamb, this time being more careful. He looked at me for a moment, then turned and charged. Just as he reached me, I threw all my weight at him. We tumbled in a mass of wool, hooves, boots, and twine. Somehow he ended up on top, but I had my hands around his mid section. He had his whole body right on top of my face.

I felt like I was being smothered to death by a giant wool pillow, but I held on as he kicked and bleated. We finally rolled over, and I was on top. I lay on him, stuck my twine around him, looped the string through itself, and I had myself a lamb.

I scrambled up, and the men all cheered. The lamb jumped up and took off running, jerking me flat on my face, dragging me a couple of feet through the muck.

Old Mr. Brown opened the gate. "Darndest thing I ever did see. Well, just point him in the right direction, and maybe he can drag you home."

I didn't plan to have him drag me home. I jumped to my feet, and we came flying out of the docking pen, my feet hardly touching the ground. That little lamb could surely run. When we reached the gate, I turned to go toward home, and the lamb turned toward the sheep pen.

There we stood, his little feet planted and mine dug in, each pulling the opposite way. I was a little bigger, so we slowly began to move my direction. I realized it would be a long process getting this stubborn wool ball home.

It seemed like it took a year just to get to the road. I decided I would have to get behind him and drive him, but if I gave him any slack, he headed toward the sheep pen. So I gave a big tug and jumped behind him. I thought the fences along each side of the road would force him to run straight ahead.

He only ran a short distance then turned and headed for the fence. The fence, built for cows, had four strands of barbed wire and no mesh.

He towed me full force into the barbed wire. "Burr Magnet!" I yelled. I don't know what it means, but it made me feel better.

I didn't know what to do. I couldn't let go of the rope, or the lamb would be back at the sheep pen before I could say "you old ewe, you" and I couldn't move, because the barbs had wrapped through my clothes, sticking me to the fence, like bramble berry burrs in cotton wool.

I tied him to one of the wires. He stretched out the twine, but it held while I untangled myself from the wire. I sat down to think.

How would I drag this little wool mule all the way home? No idea came, so I untied the twine, pulled the little lamb back to the road, and continued on. He planted all four feet and pulled against me. I put the twine around me, but I felt I was being cut in two.

I became mad, reached down, and jerked one hoof off of the ground. He stumbled forward. He couldn't pull against me as much on only three legs.

That gave me an idea. I picked up both of the lamb's front hooves. He couldn't pull against me on just his back hooves, and we started making progress toward home. He tried to nip me, so I spread his legs wide so he couldn't reach me with his teeth.

It must have looked like I was square dancing with a lamb. We could call it the Lamba Walk and maybe I could teach it to others and it could become popular. But, of course, everyone would have to get lambs... But they could do that... And I would become rich and... It was a long walk home, and my mind wandered a bit.

A half mile is a long way to walk holding onto a lamb's hooves. We stopped to rest quite often. It must have taken us at least an hour, because two cars went by, and there are never more than two cars in any given hour on the road. My dad says it's some kind of unspoken rule in the country. Except during fishing season, when he says the dust never settles.

Most people will wave and honk as they pass. One car had a bunch of smartalecky teenagers who yelled, "I think your girl friend needs to shave!"

Finally we made it home. I pulled my lamb around to the garden to find my mother.

"What have you been doing?" she asked. "And where did you get that lamb?"

When I told her how Old Mr. Brown had given him to me, she asked, "What's wrong with him?"

I told her I was sure there was nothing wrong with him.

"Well, you lock him in the barn and I'll get a bottle of milk ready."

I put him in the newborn calf pen. It was the one place I thought he couldn't get out of.

There were no newborn calves right then, so he had it all to himself. I had a hard time getting the twine off. When I finally did, he turned and gave me a quick kick in the shin as he darted off.

When I stepped into the house, Mom covered her nose.

"You are not going around smelling like that. You change your clothes; the milk is nearly warm."

3

A Lamb Named Nosey

The lamb bottle was simply an old pop bottle fitted with a rubber nipple. My mom funneled the warmed milk into it.

I ran all the way to the barn, but the calf pen was empty. He must have gone through the slatted fence, but I was sure he had to be in the barn. All of the doors were closed.

I heard a sound coming from the milking area. Sure enough, it was my lamb. There was a small opening in the cinder block wall, only big enough for a cat to slip through. My lamb had his head stuck in it. He was too big to go forward, and he couldn't come back because his ears were too wide.

I tried to pull him out, but he kicked at me. I thought the front end would be safer. I went outside and around the barn to where his head was sticking out. As I pushed the bottle nipple into his mouth, he tried to ram me. I was glad he was stuck.

I couldn't get him to open his mouth. He clamped his teeth shut, and when I put the nipple up to his mouth, he tried to bite me.

I remembered a trick my dad used on our horse to get her to open her mouth so he could put a bridle on her. I grabbed the lamb around the nose with my fingers and pressed really hard just behind the back teeth. This forced his mouth open just a little, and I shoved the bottle nipple in.

He flipped his head, which made me lose my grip, and sprayed me with milk. But he had tasted it. He licked his lips, and when I put the nipple up to his mouth again, he opened it a tiny bit. I got a little milk in his mouth before he jerked away. He licked his lips again, and when I put the bottle up to his mouth the next time, he didn't pull away at all. He sucked hard, and drained the whole bottle. I petted his head, and he nuzzled against my hand. I even let him suck on my fingers, but then he bit me when he didn't get any milk out of them.

I stayed there all afternoon, talking to him and petting him.

"What should I name you?" I asked. He just baaed at me. "I could name you Fluffy," I suggested. Somehow Fluffy sounded like a girl's name, and besides, he seemed too tough to be called Fluffy. "How about 'Lamb,' or 'Whitey,' or 'Skip'?" I asked. My lamb just baaed his disapproval of all of those names.

"How about Mutton?" a voice behind me said.

I turned around to see Daniel.

"Why Mutton?" I asked.

"Because mutton is a sheep roast."

"No!" I hollered. "This is my lamb, and he's not going to be a roast!"

Daniel looked disgusted. "Fat chance."

"Mr. Brown calls him Burr Magnet," I told him.

Daniel smiled at that. His smile widened when he saw my lamb's ears wedged against the cinder blocks. "How did he get his head stuck?"

"He was trying to escape. Can you help me get him out?"

"Sure. I'll just go get a saw and we'll cut his head off."

I shook my head and tried to act brave, even though I couldn't think of any other way to get him free. Daniel must have been teasing though, because he laughed.

He petted my lamb. "You're sure a cute little guy. But you've got to be careful sticking your nose into places it doesn't belong." Suddenly Daniel's face lit up. "That's it! We can call him Nosey."

I didn't like that name, but I had to admit it fit. So Nosey it was.

Daniel ran his hand along Nosey's head. "Now, let's see if we can get you out of there, little feller."

He gently pulled Nosey's head forward with one hand, and then, with the other, he tucked Nosey's ears against his neck. He then pushed Nosey's head back through the wall, and the lamb was free.

"Why don't you go get him another bottle of milk while I get the cows in?" Daniel suggested.

Mom fixed another bottle, and I hurried back to the barn. This time, Nosey didn't run away from me. He didn't get too close, but he didn't run away. I held the bottle out as far as I could reach, then inched toward him. He seemed ready to run away at any moment. Stretching his head out as well, he barely touched the bottle.

He licked it a few times and tried to get his mouth on it without moving. Then something scared him and he ran away. Again, I held the bottle out as far as I could reach. He stretched his neck out and barely licked the nipple. Finally we got close enough that he could get the whole thing in his mouth, and he gulped it down.

I needed to get him out of the milking area so we could milk the cows. I used the bottle to lead him into the milk room, but Nosey ran away whenever we got close to the door.

Daniel helped me corner him. As he was reaching for him, Nosey charged. Daniel scooped him up. "Spunky little feller, isn't he?"

We got him back in the newborn calf pen, and blocked any holes we found. Daniel opened the door to the barn and started driving the cows in. While I was watching the cows, Nosey disappeared. I was scared that he might get hurt. I started calling him as loud as I could.

Once all of the cows were in the barn, Daniel shut the door. Just then, Bossy, our orneriest cow, bellowed and jumped, kicking out with her back hooves. Nosey, the master milk stealer, had tried to find dessert. Bossy's hooves connected, and Nosey came flying across the barn like a drop-kicked, fuzzy white football. He had no sooner landed than another cow bellowed and kicked, sending him through the air again. From cow to cow they kicked him like a soccer ball.

"They'll kill him!" I yelled.

"Nah," Daniel said, "but the little fur ball will learn a lesson."

Nosey darted here and there, as hooves were striking at him from all directions. Finally, he slid under the gate, and Daniel swept him into his arms. Nosey was breathing hard as Daniel handed him to me, and he didn't fight. I took him back into the newborn calf pen and petted him. I got him some fresh straw and made him a bed, and he nuzzled me.

My other brothers and sisters heard I had a lamb, and they came to see him. He didn't like the attention and hid in the corner. When someone would get too close, he would charge at them. Everyone laughed because he acted so tough. When we left, we shut the barn up tight so he couldn't escape.

The next morning, I ate as fast as I could. Mom got a bottle ready, and I ran out to feed Nosey. He wasn't in the newborn calf pen, but he hadn't escaped from the barn. As I approached with his bottle, he moved toward me slowly. When the bottle nipple touched his mouth, he went after it hungrily. As he ate, I reached out my hand and stroked his soft, woolly back.

When he finished, he followed me back into the calf pen. Dad was getting the cows in for milking. "Why don't you give your lamb some bottles of water with just a little milk in it?" Dad suggested. "Don't give him too much milk, though, or you might make him sick."

I got him a bottle of warm water and added a little milk. He sucked hard at first, but finished it slowly. I got him another one, and he drank a little, but soon he would just flip the nipple with his nose. His little belly looked like an oversized water balloon. As he followed me around, waddling, I could hear sloshing in his stomach.

When chores were done, I asked Dad if I could stay and play with Nosey.

He shook his head. "No. Everyone has to get ready for school and work, and no one can stay with you."

"Can I take Nosey to play outside?"

"The lamb needs to stay in the barn, at least until he knows this is home."

I reluctantly followed everyone to the house.

I called for Tippy, and we played a game of tug-of-war with an old string. When I let go of the string, Tippy growled and jerked it around as if he had just killed some giant snake. When he got tired of that, he started chasing his tail around and around until he was dizzy. He sat down, panting.

I snuck up behind him and carefully held his tail. When he saw it, he

growled. With me holding it, he was able to grab it. He bit down hard, then yelped.

I laughed. "You are such a dough-head!" I helped him catch his tail lots of times, but he never seemed to learn.

As we played, Nosey came lumbering up, having escaped from the barn. Tippy bounced over to him. Nosey charged, but still being full of water, his charge was more like a fast waddle. However, he caught Tippy right in the chest and sent him rolling.

Tippy laid there for a minute; then he came at Nosey again. Again Nosey caught him in the chest and sent him rolling. The next time Tippy came sneaking up, he came low, on his belly. Nosey didn't like it and charged. When Nosey was almost on him, Tippy sprang, and down they rolled.

Tippy growled, and Nosey baa'd. Tippy would go off a ways, trying to get Nosey to chase him. Finally, Nosey got the idea and off they went. It wasn't long before they came back, but Tippy was chasing Nosey. I thought I would join them. Away we went, around the apple tree, under the clothesline, and through the flower bed, just as Mom opened the door.

"What is going on here?"

"We're playing tag," I answered.

"Not in my flower bed, you don't. You take that lamb and that dumb mutt and get out of there."

It seemed as the days went by that we were always in trouble for something, especially Nosey, who decided he liked to eat Mom's flowers. Daniel even made up a rhyme about us.

Tommy has a little lamb; its fleece is white as snow.
He drug it home from Brown's one day because it wouldn't go.
It pulls clothes from the line and stomps them oh so bad.
It eats Mom's flowers, messes on them, and makes her very mad
Mom swears that if he does it one more time, that lamb it will be toast.
She says, for dinner on that night, we'll have a mutton roast.

One day I decided that it would be safer for us to play in the front yard, away from Mom's flowers. We had just laid down there to rest when a car came speeding by. In an instant, Tippy jumped up and raced after it, barking. Nosey followed after him, baaing. They chased the car over the hill, then came back and flopped down beside me.

After a while, another car came, and away they raced, barking and baaing. But this time the car slowed down as the people stared out the window and pointed at Nosey. The next car stopped completely. The people ignored Tippy, but they pointed and laughed at Nosey.

The stopped car seemed to confuse Tippy. He was trying to chase the car away, and it wasn't scared. He sat down and looked back at me for help. He didn't know what to do with one if he caught it. He sniffed the car for a minute, and seemed to get an idea. He raised his leg and marked it as one he had already caught. The car sped off.

Every day after that, Nosey and Tippy chased cars. Nosey stayed a good distance off the road, but Tippy would get up very close to them. Mom said I needed to stop him or he would get run over. I tried, but it was no use. The two of them would take off after a car, and I would run after them yelling.

Daniel saw me and yelled, "Give it up! You're embarrassing us! It only looks like three idiots chasing cars instead of two!"

4

Super Cowboy Rides

Winter had been long, and the only good part of winter is Christmas. I really like magic. Flying reindeer and being able to go down a chimney is about as cool as it can get.

Last Christmas, I had decided that I was going to learn how Santa did it. I found a ladder and dragged it to the side of the house. I was just climbing up when Mom found me.

"What do you think you're doing?"

"I'm going to go up and come down the chimney like Santa does."

"You most definitely are not! It's dangerous!"

"But Santa does it," I reminded her.

"Santa is magical."

I realized that was true. But for someone who is magical, there are things I still wonder about. Santa never seems to bring anything but clothes. I think that for a guy that has a workshop full of elves making toys, he sure doesn't make many. He only has one elf that seems to get any work done, and his name is JC Penney. And all he seems to make is clothes. The reason I know this is that for as long as I can remember, there has always been a tag on the clothes from Santa with that written on it. I can't read, so I asked my dad what it said and what it was. That is when he told me it was the name of the elf that made them. He said that elves often put tags with their name on things they make.

I can tell you, I have about had it with him just making clothes for me. I have made up my mind that I am going to write JC Penney next year when I write Santa, and I am going to tell him to get with the program.

But there had been one exciting thing last Christmas. I got a cowboy hat, cowboy boots, a cowboy shirt with lots of fringe, and a scarf.

That's what I was wearing as I headed outside into the spring breeze. Mom only let me wear them in the house, saying I would get them dirty. But winter had been long, and I just had to show my new clothes to Tippy and Nosey. Besides, they made me feel kind of like Superman and a cowboy at the same time. That's why I called myself Super Cowboy.

But it's pretty hard to be Super Cowboy with milking clothes on. I don't think real cowboys even work with cows - the milking kind, anyway. Cowboys just sort of chase them on horses and all. In fact, I don't think they even chase milk cows at all. It's not exciting to chase something with a big udder swinging side to side as it walks. I figure real cowboys only chase mean, tough, ornery critters that have long horns and turn on a person if they have half a chance. Our cows seldom turn on anyone, but plod along like overgrown, cud-chewing moo-rons. That's what Daniel calls them. "Moo-rons."

I made sure Mom wasn't looking, then I hurried out. Tippy and Nosey were there to meet me, and I showed them how neat my clothes were. They didn't seem impressed, so I decided to make my way out to the milking barn.

I marched, with my head held high, and Tippy and Nosey by my side. I loved the marks my cowboy boots made in the soft dirt. They leave an imprint shaped like the boots, with a deep hole where the heel sinks. I swaggered along, straining my knees outward so I would have the bowed legs of a real cowboy.

I walked across the cement and clomped my boots as loudly as I could. I didn't have any spurs, so I had to lift my feet high, like a prancing horse. I walked into the milking barn, and Daniel and Jason, my second oldest brother, laughed.

"What's so funny?" I asked.

"Well, if it isn't Super Cowboy," Daniel snickered. "How would Super Cowboy like to ride a cow?"

I know cowboys don't ride cows. They will sometimes ride a bull, but bulls are mean, tough, and ornery. They make a worthy opponent. But riding a cow, especially the milking kind, is like picking a fight with a girl. You can't brag if you win, and you're miserably ashamed if you lose.

I turned to make a mad dash for the house. I wasn't clomping now. It didn't make any difference, though, because they caught me.

I started screaming like a pig headed for the slaughter. I was not going to give in without a fight. I kicked out and caught Daniel with a pointed boot, but he acted like it hardly fazed him; although, with my great Super Cowboy strength, I know he must have been greatly wounded. Daniel stuck me on top of a big, black and white Holstein that had her head in the stanchion and was being milked.

Milking cows, for the most part, are really quite gentle. But they don't like to be considered a leather chair. This cow bellered like an old tractor pulling a plow, and she slammed back against the stanchion that was holding her. She kept leaping forward and slamming back - her bellering, and me screaming and holding onto her skin. Milk cows don't even have decent skin to hold onto.

My brothers were bent over with laughter, tears rolling from their eyes. They didn't even see the block that held the cow in the stall wiggling loose. With each lunge, the block wiggled a little more, and the cow became angrier. With each lunge, my head snapped back and forth. Then, with one final lunge, the block slipped free.

The cow whirled, and I was barely able to hold on. Snorting snot from her nostrils like a fire-breathing dragon, she plastered the walls, the other cows, and my brothers. Foam was coming from her mouth as if she were a rabid dog. Her sides were heaving. She was bellowing to let everyone who dared challenge her know they were taking their life into their hands. Angrily she headed for the open door.

My brothers, who weren't laughing now, tried to head her off. The milker was still attached to her and the hoses stretched tight like a rubber band before it popped loose, flying back and smashing into the wall.

I was lying down now with my arms and legs wrapped around her as if I was hugging an oversized bear. Daniel grabbed her tail and began skiing down the barn alley, throwing a manure wave higher than his waist. Jason gallantly tried to jump in her path with a stick.

The cow was determined to be free. She made a quick twist, sidestepping Jason. The twisting of her body threw Daniel, who was still holding onto her tail, leaving him in a tangle of arms and legs in the manure with Jason.

Now that the cow was past them, she began to run in a jumping, seesawing motion. I began going up and down like a Raggedy Andy doll, with my chin smashing into the cow's backbone. I was too frightened to stay on and way too terrified to jump off. She was headed straight for the manure pit. I thought she would run directly into it, throwing manure clear over her back, like a race car going through a mud puddle. But this was not a dumb cow. Just inches before she reached the manure pit, she turned, launching me into the air like a rock from a cow-tapult.

It's amazing how many things go through one's mind while sailing through the air, headed for a three-foot-deep, wet manure pit. It isn't near as much as the stuff that goes through a person's nose, ears, and mouth when they hit, but a few choice thoughts about my brothers did enter in.

I went in head first, hit bottom, and skidded along the cement pad for a short distance, three feet under a pool of green slime.

I immediately thought I was going to drown. Then I felt a hand on my boots, and I came out, head down, as if I were a newborn baby calf. I could see the cow, bounding off across the corral, her udder pounding side to side, as she bellered to tell the other cows of the insult and injustice she had just been subjected to. I was dripping green slime out of my mouth, nose, ears, and boots and ...

"Oh, no! My cowboy boots! You guys have ruined my cowboy boots!" I yelled. "I hate you! I am never going to speak to you again!"

My brothers looked at me solemnly, then Daniel got a mischievous smile and said, "Promises, promises, promises." They busted out laughing as they stuck me right side up on the cement.

"With a bath like that, you won't have to bathe for a month," Daniel said.

"More like he will have to stay in the bath for a month," Jason said. "Hey, it's the Jolly Green Giant."

"Or maybe the Jolly Green Super Cowboy," Daniel said.

That was it. My cowboy boots were ruined. My scarf was ruined. My shirt was slimy and torn, and my hat was still floating in three feet of manure. I started yelling.

"You think it's funny! You just wait until I tell Mom and Dad you stuck me on a wild cow and deliberately tried to kill me!"

They did seem scared about that. Before they let me go to the house, they sprayed me down with a hose. They washed out my ears, nose, and mouth, but the horrible taste wouldn't leave. They did everything they could to calm me and make things look better for them when they had to face our parents.

I marched straight to the house. All the way, my boots went, "squish, squish" instead of "clomp, clomp," making me madder and madder. I banged so hard on the door with my fist that I felt like my hand would break.

Mom finally opened the door. Some wind blew past me and Mom took a quick step back. I started to step in and she stepped back into the doorway, blocking my path.

"Oh, no, you don't, young man. You are not putting one foot in this house smelling like that. Where in the world have you been?"

I looked at my torn and dirty clothes, caught a whiff of my own smell, and with what little pride I had left, said, "Jason and Daniel tried to kill me by making me ride the orneriest, toughest cow in the whole herd."

5

Buttercups And Party Lines

It was almost summer, and I was really bored and wanted something to do. My older brothers and sisters were still in school, and the radio was broken.

I had seen the yellow flowers called buttercups blooming all through the pasture, so I decided I would pick a whole wagon full of them for Mom. I found my little red wagon, and I called for Tippy and Nosey. They came running, and we set out across the pasture.

Here and there, on the north side of the machinery that had been parked in the pasture, there were still small piles of snow. With most of the snow now gone, this snow was more valuable. It was fun to get a snowball and sneak up on someone and let them have it.

I grabbed a big chunk of ice to suck on off of an old combine as I crossed the pasture. Jason told me I shouldn't suck on them because birds pooped on the machinery, and the water washing off is what formed the icicles. He thinks just because I am young I will believe anything. I couldn't see any bird poop in the ice.

There was a meadow that looked like a big lake of yellow where the flowers grew. I ran out into the middle of it and took a deep breath. Besides the flowers, I could also smell the mint that grew along the ditch banks. I closed my eyes and enjoyed the smells.

Soon I had filled the whole wagon full of yellow buttercups and dandelions. I knew I should start back, but the perfume of the flowers and warmth of the sun made me sleepy, and I wanted to lie down.

I flopped down on my back, and watched the clouds rolling a picture show across the giant blue sky. Tippy chased butterflies not too far away, and I could hear the munch, munch of Nosey eating grass by my feet. The world became quieter and quieter.

Suddenly, I felt a blast of warm air, and a slimy drizzle on my face that made me gag. As I awoke, a cow scraped her rough tongue across my face. I screamed, and the cows scattered, bellowing and stumbling. They tipped over my little red wagon, as they headed to the far side of the pasture as a thundering herd.

The sun was no longer straight overhead, and I was hungry. I set my little red wagon upright, gathered up the flowers, and put them back in. Someone called my name.

I called back, and Albert and Daniel came running. Albert was first to reach me, and he acted real important.

"Look who I found," he bragged to Daniel.

They pulled me and my little red wagon back to the house, spilling out most of the flowers as we went.

Mom was almost frantic. "Where the devil have you been? We have the whole neighborhood out hunting for you!"

I don't know why she was so worried. I knew where I was the whole time. All she had to do was ask.

Once I was back the house, I became bored again. I would usually spend my free time with Tippy and Nosey. But sometimes I want something else to do. With our radio broken, we had nothing to listen to. We had an old TV that an uncle gave us, but it only worked off and on - mostly off.

We had a telephone, but since we lived far out in the country, we had what everyone called a party line. I think that is a real strange thing to call it, because I can't see how anyone can use it to party. I asked my mom about it, and she said a party line meant that several people shared the same phone line. "It is only for very important things, and you must never, never touch it," she warned me. "Especially when it isn't our ring."

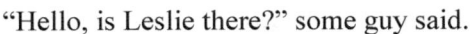

I understood some about the rings. There were times when it would ring and someone would say, "That isn't our ring. Just leave it alone." And other times when it would ring, someone would say, "That's our ring. Someone better get it."

I was never allowed to use the phone, and that just made me more curious, especially when it rang and we weren't supposed to touch it. I was in the kitchen, wishing for something to do, when the phone rang with one of the "other" rings. No one was around, and I was curious, so I got a chair and pulled it from off of the wall. I heard two voices on it.

"Hello, is Leslie there?" some guy said.

"This is her," a girl's voice answered.

"Hi, Leslie," the guy's voice said. "This is Jack."

"Oh, Jack," Leslie's voice said, "I'm so glad you called. I was really wanting to talk to you."

There were some radio programs my mom wouldn't let us listen to. She said they weren't appropriate. I wondered if the rings that weren't for us were like that. Maybe Mom didn't want me to listen because it was one of those mushy programs she always made me shut off. I was more convinced of this as Jack asked Leslie to go with him to the movies.

"Oh, I'd love to go," Leslie said.

"The plot sickens," I said. I didn't know what it meant, but that's what Daniel always says just before Mom makes us shut it off.

"Is there somebody on this line?" Leslie asked.

This was a new twist to the radio I didn't quite understand. It was almost as if I was part of the program. I thought that was neat. I decided to see if I truly was. "It's me," I said.

"Well, you better get off, if you know what's good for you," she threatened.

Was this like radio or not? Leslie's voice sounded like that of the teenage neighbor girl. I wondered if I maybe I was using the phone wrong. I thought I would do what my Mom and Dad did when they first picked up the phone. I started clicking the little handle up and down and saying, "Hello? Hello? Is anyone there?"

"Knock that off. Of course we're here, you little twerp," Leslie said, the emotion rising in her voice. "I just told you to get off of the phone. Get off now, or I'm going to pound you to a pulp!"

I thought if this was like a radio, with the tension building, there should be scary music.

Jack's voice came back on. "Now, Leslie," he said. "He just sounds like a little kid that doesn't know better. Be nice. Here, let me try. How old are you?"

"I'm five."

"See," Leslie fumed. "It's the little neighbor twerp."

"No," I protested, "I'm not a twerp. I'm a Johnson."

Jack laughed. I don't know why he laughed, but something must have been funny. His laugh made me laugh, too.

That really made Leslie mad. "Wait until I get hold of you!" she yelled. Then she said some things I thought weren't supposed to be said on a radio, especially by a girl.

"If I talked that way," I said, "my mother would wash my mouth out with soap."

Jack laughed again, so I laughed.

Leslie said a few more things that sounded like the way Mr. Brown talks. I was afraid Mom might come along and find out I was listening to that kind of thing, so I thought I'd better change the channel. The only thing on the phone to change the channel was a circular dial with little holes in it, so I put my finger in the holes and turned it, like I had seen my parents do. This made an interesting clickety-clicking sound as the little wheel went around.

"Quit dialing, you moron," Leslie yelled. "Can't you see we're on the phone?"

"Nope, I can't see you," I answered.

Jack laughed again, so I laughed.

"I like this little guy," Jack said. "He's pretty sharp."

I didn't know what it meant to be sharp, but the way Jack said it, I knew it was good. Leslie didn't seem to have the same opinion. "Maybe we should get back together when we can have some privacy," she said.

"Sure," Jack replied.

They each said goodbye. Then there was a strange clicking sound, and then it buzzed. It sounded like our radio did when we weren't getting a channel - just a steady buzzing sound, and no music or talking coming out. I tried clicking the handle on the phone. I tried changing the channel, but it only went to a steady beeping, then went quiet. I figured something must have gone wrong with it, so I quickly put it back before someone came along and blamed me for breaking it.

After that, I realized that if the phone rang that same ring, I could pick it up, and it was almost always Leslie and Jack. On the radio, I always knew when a certain program was coming on by the music. On the phone, it was obviously the ring that told a person who was on.

I began to like Jack more and more, and Leslie less and less. He was always nice to me, and she was always mean. Then one day, there was another guy on the phone.

"Hello," the man's voice said. "Is Leslie there?"

"This is her," I heard Leslie say in the sweet voice I had come to recognize at the first of these conversations. The reason I say at the first is because, as they went on, she always got madder and madder, and her voice was not as soft.

"This is Robert," the man's voice said.

"Oh, Robert," Leslie said. "I'm so glad you called. I was really hoping to talk to you."

"Robert?" I asked. "What happened to Jack?"

"Jack?" Robert asked.

"Get off the phone," Leslie demanded, her voice no longer sweet. I thought that was about the fastest I had heard her voice go from sweet to mad.

"Jack?" Robert asked again.

"Yeah, Jack," I answered.

"Who's Jack?"

"Jack is nobody," Leslie answered.

"I like Jack," I said. "He is always nice to me."

"Who's Jack?" Robert asked again.

"Jack is the other guy she always talks to," I explained.

"Is that so? That wouldn't happen to be Jack Dayton, would it?" Robert asked.

"I don't know," I answered. "He just goes by Jack."

"You little twerp," Leslie fumed. "You better get off of this phone, or I'm going to break every bone in your..."

"Wait a minute," Robert interrupted. "Is it Jack Dayton, or isn't it?"

"Yes," Leslie replied quietly.

"Well, Leslie, Jack is one of my good friends. I can't be asking you out or anything if you are going out with Jack."

"I'm not anymore," Leslie said.

"Yip. Just a two-timin' woman," I sing-songed into the phone. I didn't know what it meant, but John sang it when his girlfriend went out with another guy.

"Why, you rotten little jerk!" Leslie shouted.

Suddenly, I heard my mother's voice behind me. "Tommy, what are you doing?"

"Just listening to the phone," I said.

My mom put out her hand for the phone, and I reluctantly gave it to her. Then she spoke into it, "Is anyone on here?"

Suddenly, I could hear some shouting of some things that I think would have even embarrassed Mr. Brown. I saw my mom blush and hold the phone away from her ear. I thought, "Boy, is Leslie going to be in trouble." But instead, all my mom said was, "I see. I will take care of it." She then hung up the phone, and, boy, did she ever take care of it. I thought my backside would be sore forever.

I went out and found Tippy and Nosey, and we went to sit on the haystack so I could feel sorry for myself. "There just isn't any justice in the world," I complained to them. "Leslie is the one that says all those bad things, and I'm the one that gets in trouble." I knew it wouldn't do any good to talk to a grownup about how unfair it was. Whenever I told my dad that something wasn't fair, he would just say, "Well, that's life. Get used to it." I always wondered why it couldn't be unfair in my favor once in a while.

After a while, I heard someone calling my name. I didn't even want to answer. But as they continued to call, I decided I better go, because my backside was already sore.

When I got to the house, I was told there was a package for me. I opened it up, and there was a great, big candy bar inside.

There was a note with it, so Mom read it to me. It said, "To Tommy. Thanks for helping us be smart. Your friends, Jack and Robert."

"Who are Jack and Robert?" my mom asked.

"Oh, just a couple of friends from the telephone," I answered, with a mouth already full of chocolate.

6

Tarzan

Our barn is one of the tall ones that seems to go forever into the sky. I like the musty smell of grain dust, straw, and old hay, and I enjoy sitting and daydreaming. I usually dream about being an astronaut, a cowboy, or Superman.

There is an area above the milking parlor that is filled with grain. To feed the cows during the milking, bins extend down within two feet of the floor. It has a board with a handle that fits into a slot in the bin. When we pull the board, grain drops to the cows.

One of my jobs is to make sure the grain bins are full before each milking. When I finish, I like to flop onto the straw bales and look at the sun twinkling through the roof where a shingle is missing here and there.

The barn has two angles in the roof. On the inside, where the two angles meet, there is a small ledge. Pigeons build nests there. I always collect a few feathers from the ground below to pretend I am an Indian. Sometimes I use them trying to fly.

The barn has a big ladder inside at the back end that goes up to a huge opening. There the roof of the barn goes out a ways beyond the back of the barn. There is a steel rail that runs along the top of the barn, all the way out the back overhang.

I like to climb up to the opening and swing one leg over the wall to sit and enjoy the view. The land behind our barn is mostly flat. There are the sheep sheds, and then a wide expanse of rangeland covered with sagebrush and brush grass.

Across the wide rangeland there is an occasional clump of trees. These grow around small pools of water.

The farthest thing I can see from the back of the barn is the juniper mountains. The juniper mountains aren't really mountains, and Dad says they don't really have any name, but we call them "The Junipers." I'm sure it is because they are covered with short, straggly juniper trees.

The front of the barn also has a ladder up to the top to a very small doorway, one that is only big enough for a single person. I just lean out this one, because I never feel safe sitting on the high, small ledge.

The metal rail that runs along the top of the barn out to the back overhang is old and rusty. My dad said that in the days of the horse and buggy, they would run hay from a big fork thing along the rail and then drop it on the stack. Now we just stack about 500 bales of straw there. The old wooden fork isn't there anymore, except for a few rotted boards, but the metal wheel part is still connected to the rail. It just hangs, old and motionless, except for an occasional breeze that makes it rock back and forth.

There are big wooden beams that run across the barn between the two sides of the roof. A few weeks after my scary cow ride, Albert and I got a rock and tied a string around it, and tried to throw it over one of these beams to make a rope swing. Albert was first to try. He threw forever.

"Let me have a turn," I said.

"You're too little," he answered.

"Am not."

"Are too."

"Am not."

"Okay. I'll give you one shot," he said.

Mine went up and just dinged the beam - closer than any of his. Since he had been in school, I had spent hours throwing rocks at posts, trees, cans, and anything else I could take aim at. I had become quite good, and could hit them most of the time. However, the rock bounced back and barely missed us.

"See, you nearly killed us," he said.

"At least I hit the beam," I countered.

"Yeah, but you're not supposed to hit the beam. You're supposed to go over it."

"Well, your shots haven't even come close."

"That's because I didn't try," he replied.

Albert didn't try again for something like a million times, until I thought I was going to die of boredom. He wasn't going to let me try because he was afraid I might actually do it.

Finally, he got the idea to stack up the bales so we would be closer. We stacked them into stairs until it was pretty high. Of course, he had to be the one to try it.

He was on the top bale that wobbled on top of two others. He drew back and threw the rock toward the beam. It hit the top of the barn, and ended up going over the beam. However, as he threw it, the bale rolled out from under him, and he came bouncing down the pile we had stacked up. I tried to jump clear of his arms, but I was too slow, and he caught me across the middle, tumbling me into the grain pile.

I love the smell of grain with molasses rolled sweetly into it, but I hate it in my hair and underpants. It itches and scratches, like being licked all over by sandpaper. I was laying there in the grain, looking up at the barn roof, with its little rays of light shining through, wondering what it would have been like to be an only child.

The wind was knocked out of me, and I began to itch like I had a rash. Despite my misery, the memory of his feet flipping out from under him and coming up past his head as he tumbled down the straw stack made me laugh. He jumped up, mad, ready to smack me, when he saw that the rope was over the beam.

"You think it's funny, huh?" he snorted. "Well, the rope is over the beam, and since I got it there, that means the swing belongs to me."

"That's fine. I'll throw up my own rope," I said.

"Since mine was there first, that means I own the beam. You can't put one up there without my permission," he said.

There are times I truly have wished I was an only child, and there are other times I have felt like making myself one person closer to it. This was one of those times.

We both knew it would still take a lot of work to get the rope where we needed it. It was only a few inches over the beam, and we couldn't pull it, because it would just come back over the top. The only thing we could do is to wiggle it a little at a time and hope it would work its way down.

Albert began to whip the rope back and forth. Little by little, the rock, with the rope attached, started inching its way to the floor. He whipped it a little too much, and the rock came flying out of the string. When it did, the rope flipped back over the beam, falling to his feet.

I laughed, jumped up and down, and shouted, "I guess the beam isn't yours any more!"

He pushed me off the straw pile into the itchy grain again.

He wasn't about to do his somersault another time. "We will have to pile up more straw," he informed me. "I am tired from throwing the rock over, so I am afraid you will have to be the one to stack up the straw."

I looked at him and rolled my eyes. "Why should I? You think it's your beam, and your swing, and your barn, and your farm, and your world. You give me one good reason that I should?"

"Because I will give you the first swing," he said.

"You promise?"

"I promise."

"I'm not sure that is good enough."

"I'm also tougher than you, and could hurt you pretty bad," he added.

I started hauling the straw up the stack, wishing he weren't my brother. I finally got the top of the stack so it didn't wobble. As he prepared to throw, I moved far away from the edge, so I wouldn't be hit by anybody coming down. This time he didn't hit it on his first shot, but it didn't take him too long. Once we had both ends of the string, I excitedly stepped forward to take my turn.

"Okay. I'm ready to go!"

"Right after me," he answered, pushing me out of the way.

"But you said I could go first."

"Yeah. You will be the first person to go right after me."

"I hope the rope breaks." I mumbled.

"What was that?"

"Nothin'."

It wasn't a fancy rope like our cousins have in their barn. I can put my hand around theirs, and barely touch finger tip to finger tip. Our rope, on the other hand, wasn't truly a rope at all. It was just some twine off of hay bales. It was slick, and the strands that stuck out would cut us if we slid our hands along it.

We planned to do like we had always done at our cousins' house. We would swing down off the big pile of straw, feeling the rush of the wind. Some of the older cousins would swing their legs up and arch their back as they came back to the straw stack, and land right back up on top. I tried this many times, but have never been able to do it. I always crash into the stack.

There is one thing we forgot about in all of this. Our cousins' straw stack was at one end of the barn, and their rope was in the middle. Our rope was in the middle, but so was the straw stack we built to throw the rope over. Albert grabbed the rope tight like we always had at our cousins' house; he did a dying cow impersonation of Tarzan, then he jumped. He hardly went anywhere; he just dangled in mid air not far from the straw stack.

"Having fun?" I smirked.

"Shut up and pull me in," he growled.

"Look, everyone," I mumbled. "I caught a fish. No, I think it's just a sucker. I will probably have to throw it back, or maybe just throw it away."

"What are you muttering about?" he asked.

"Nothing."

"It better be nothing!"

He acted all grown up and smart as he talked. "The problem is we didn't consider the finer points of mathematics. I just didn't give myself enough slack to swing, that's all."

"I don't remember having much slack in the rope in Uncle Darren's barn," I replied.

"That's because you are little and don't remember the finer details."

I still didn't remember jumping off with any slack in the rope, but he gave himself a lot of slack and jumped off. He headed straight down the stack. His legs hit the floor first, and the rope got just enough tension at the last minute to keep him from sinking his nose through the floor.

I was suddenly very happy that he wanted to go first. I laughed until I had a side ache. Although he lay there for some time, somehow he found enough energy to come up and push me off the stack again.

"I have another plan," he said. "You need to move the straw down to the end of the barn."

"Why me?" I asked.

"Because I got hurt," he answered.

"You didn't look hurt when you pushed me off of the straw stack."

He gave me one of those, 'I don't want any more out of you' looks, and I started to haul the straw. I knew I would have to hurry because it was almost milking time. I worked hard and the sweat mixed with grain dust on my face. He began to hum; to make fun of me, I'm sure. Finally, although it was not all moved, there was enough stacked at the end so we could swing. He helped pull the last few bales to the side so we had a clear path all the way to the dusty floor.

He got up on the stack, all ready to go again. I didn't even argue. I was too tired, and I thought I would wait until it was all tested. I'm sure if he thought anything could go wrong this time, he would give me the first shot. We stood high above the floor, much higher than before, since we had stacked the straw from the middle pile on top of the straw that was already at the end of the barn.

With a loud yell, he jumped. Everything worked flawlessly until he was coming to the bottom ready to turn even with the floor, and then the importance of a good rope became obvious. He started to slide down the slick rope, faster and faster, until he was flung like a skipping stone across the surface of the barn loft. He left a nice, smooth trail across the rough lumber, and finally came to rest on his back. I could just imagine all the nice slivers he had picked up.

I burst out laughing. "Wow! That was neat! Do it again! Do it again!"

He jumped up, and I knew he was mad. This time, I decided to beat it to the bottom of the stack before he pushed me there. I found I didn't have to hurry too fast, though. He could hardly move with all of those slivers sticking in his backside.

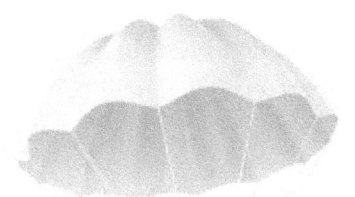

7

Parachute Inventors

Albert said he had figured a way to make tons of money creating a new and better parachute. I am not sure where he read it, because I can only look at the pictures and the pictures he showed me didn't even look like parachutes.

"Believe me," he said, "it says the government needs better parachutes for people jumping out of planes. The government pays lots of money for these kinds of things. We could be rich. Why, they may pay us as much as a hundred dollars."

A hundred dollars was a lot, so I didn't believe him. "I don't know. How can we design a parachute? We don't even have any money."

"We don't need money," he answered, "just a lot of skill. And we have the perfect parachute jump-off point. We can use the back doorway of the barn loft."

"Where are you going to get the material?" I asked.

"You leave that to me," he answered.

Albert disappeared for a while, so I decided to make use of the swing we had put up. We had all the problems worked out of it now. We couldn't just hold on to the rope because we would slide down it, so we had tied a good, strong stick at the end of the string. We actually ended up tying two. We put our feet on one stick and held onto the other. It was just about impossible to swing back up onto the straw stack like our cousins did, so we would just swing until it slowed to a stop.

Albert came back with what looked like some sheets.

"Did Mom give you those?" I asked.

"I didn't ask," he answered. "These are just some old rags that she had."

They sure looked like good sheets to me.

Albert worked his calculations. "How much do you weigh?"

"What are you asking that for?"

"So I can design the parachute exactly to your weight."

I may be young, but I'm not stupid. "If you think I am going to take one of your parachutes and jump off of the barn, you are crazy!"

"How do you expect us to make all that money if we don't test this? Somebody has to do it. With my calculations, it will be perfect. There will be absolutely nothing to worry about."

"Good. Then you can do it," I said.

"I need to stay at the top so I can watch how it works and make any minor adjustments," he answered.

"I thought you said your calculations would be perfect."

I could see by the look on his face that he was trying to figure an answer to that. He knew I was right. The wonderful job of calculating rope length for the swing was still on our minds. I knew he wasn't going to test the parachute and I also knew I wasn't.

"I have an idea," Albert said. "Didn't NASA send up a monkey in the first space ship?"

"They said so on the radio."

"Well," he said with great triumph, "We'll do that."

"You mean, get Willie to do it?" I asked.

"No, he is too little and Mom would never let us take him out of the house. I mean we can use some animal. Maybe a dog."

"Oh, no! You aren't going to use Tippy!"

"It could be any farm animal," he countered.

"Well, you can't use Nosey either. And I don't think dad would like you throwing the calves off of the barn. Besides, I don't think we can haul one up here."

He grinned. "No, but there are plenty of cats."

"Cats? They won't get hurt will they?"

"Nah, of course not. My parachutes will keep them perfectly safe."

"How are we going to catch them?"

"Hey, do I have to do everything around here?" he asked. "I got the parachute materials. You get the cats."

We didn't dare touch our sisters' pet cats. We had gotten in trouble for that before. But all of the rest of the cats were wild. We couldn't afford to feed all of the ones people dumped off on our road, so they just turned wild to survive.

They often had to fight for food. When we had a little milk left over, we would put some in a bowl just in front of the barn. We would yell, "Here kitty, kitty," and the cats would attack it like a black, gray, and orange storm cloud. Fur would fly as the cats fought for position at the milk bowl.

We also put scraps in a bowl just outside the back door of the house. I usually tried to save the best pieces for Tippy. One day, a wild cat grabbed one of the biggest ones I had saved. It took off with it as fast as it could run. I chased it, determined to get Tippy's food back.

The cat could normally outrun me, but the food slowed it down, and soon I had it cornered. As I came closer and closer, the hair on its back stood on end and a deep rattle sound came from its throat. I made a jump for the cat. I don't remember all that happened after that, but the next thing I knew, I was lying there, ripped up and bleeding. I decided then that I wouldn't tangle with one of those killer cats again.

Albert took the parachute material back and I tried to think of a way to catch cats. I had lots of time at home while he was at school. I looked at some magazines and saw a trap with a door that flopped down when an animal went inside. The animal in the picture was a raccoon, but I figured it would work on cats. I couldn't convince Mom or Dad that I needed one, so I decided that I would have to build one.

I got a cardboard box and cut a flap for a door. I had to think a long time to figure out how I would get the door to close. I finally hit on a plan. I tied a string onto the door. Then I cut a hole in the back of the box. I ran the string through the back of the box to the house where I could hide. I got some milk and put it in the box, called, "Here kitty, kitty," and then ran and hid inside the house. I kept the door of the house open just enough so I could pull the string through it.

The cats were very wary of the box. They prowled around it, smelling the milk inside. Soon, hunger overcame one, and it ventured inside. I jerked the string, and the door on the box closed with a thump. But I didn't realize how strong those cats were. He flew through the door, bending the cardboard out of his road as if it wasn't even there.

I decided I had to do something more with the door. I took a small piece of wood that was wider than the door I had cut in the box. I found some old, rusty nails, and nailed the cardboard to the wood. I again set out the milk, called the cats, and got back into my position.

The cats, more wary than before, slunk around the box, but eventually one went in. I slammed the door shut. The box began to jump around. I pulled the box over, being careful to keep the rope tight. Before I could get the cat, however, he had ripped his way through the cardboard side of the box, and was gone.

I knew then that I would have to make the whole trap out of wood. That was okay because there are always plenty of wood scraps around our farm. My problem was finding some pieces that would be the right size. I was not allowed to use saws, so I knew they would have to work the way they were. I did find two pieces that were almost perfect. The rest were only close. I nailed and pounded the box together with some half bent nails. It was probably the ugliest thing ever built.

I found an old hinge and mounted it on a board for the door. Just one hinge made the door wobbly, but I couldn't find another one. I took an old manual wood drill and drilled a hole in the back for the string to go through. All of this took me the rest of the week, but Saturday morning, bright and early after chores, Albert and I were ready to test the trap.

We put in the milk and took up positions. The cats had forgotten about the other trap and it wasn't long before one cautiously slunk inside. Albert, who had taken the string from me, jerked the door closed. The box rocked as the cat hit the sides, trying to find a way out. Albert handed me the rope. He wanted to be the first to triumphantly pull the cat from the box. I never argued. I still remembered my last run in with a wild cat.

Albert put on a glove, and I loosened the rope just enough so that he could reach his hand into the box. The cat let out a "fffftttt" and then, like a car squealing out in gravel, it started peeling out on its way up Albert's arm. It left some scratch marks all the way between the glove and his short sleeved shirt. It gave him a good scare, and he fell, panting, onto his back. He looked up at me and, suddenly, he was furious.

"This was the stupidest idea I have ever heard of! It was all your fault! You wipe that stupid smile off your face, or I'll wipe it off for you!"

He came after me, but I was too close to the door of the house. I dropped the string and ran in. He chased me all of the way into the kitchen, and we nearly bumped into Mom.

"What is the matter with you two, and Albert, what have you done to your arm?"

"A cat scratched me."

"You know I have told you two a thousand times to leave those cats alone."

Mom always exaggerates. I don't know what a thousand is, but it sounds like a lot and she says that every time.

We didn't catch any more cats that day. We decided I would try to catch some on Monday while Albert was at school. By being really patient, I was able to catch quite a few. When I had one in the trap, I would put on very thick clothing, pick up a forked stick, and open the door to the trap just a crack so I could put the stick in. The cat would always jump at the door, but it couldn't get out. I would bring the stick closer and closer to the cat. He would whack at it, but I would eventually get him pushed up against the side. I would hold him there until I could reach in with my other hand and grab him. I could always feel his claws through my gloves and thick clothing, but not enough to hurt me.

On Monday night, after school, we were ready to start our parachute trials. Albert had taken the sheets back to wherever he got them, so he had to run into the house and get them again. We had the cats in a chicken cage. Albert carefully reached in and pulled one out. He was dressed in thick clothing this time. He didn't want to take any chances.

He laid out the material, making his "exact measurements." I held the spitting, hissing victim, stretched out by its paws to keep its teeth away from me, while Albert tied the parachute to it.

We climbed up the ladder at the back of the barn, so we were both at the doorway on top. Albert cat-a-pulted the cat into the air. The parachute opened and slowed the cat's fall down for a short distance, but something went wrong. The weight was too much for it, and the parachute folded upward, letting the cat come sailing out of the sky in a furious descent. The drop wasn't that far so I don't mean the cat got hurt. I just mean the cat was furious.

Albert looked down at the cat trying to rid himself of the parachute and said, "Hurry and grab the cat while he's busy. Maybe you can even save the parachute."

I slid down the straw bales and almost dropped out of the loft hurrying down the ladder. As I came to the cat, my exuberance turned to dread as the cat turned to face me. His beady black eyes met mine, and I could see anger burning in them. He didn't even back away as I inched my way toward him, but instead he kept tearing at the parachute.

As I came closer, a deep rumble came from his throat, and he crouched into attack position. He seemed to want me to come. I froze, thinking I truly didn't want the parachute or the cat all that bad. We stood there, face to face, him crouched ready to spring, and me set ready to run. Then he did what I considered to be a very noble thing. He turned and ran like crazy across the barnyard. The parachute, now mostly in tatters, flayed out behind him. I chased after him, but not at full speed. I most certainly didn't want to catch him; I just wanted to make Albert think I tried. After a good ways of running, I returned to the loft, pretending to breathe hard to show great exertion, even though I truly wasn't tired.

Albert was annoyed. "I've seen dead cows run faster than you."

"Yeah, well, I didn't see you chasing after it."

"If you would have, you would have seen it caught."

"That's good. You can go after the next one."

"I suppose, if I have to do all the work, you won't get any of the money."

As we watched another one, two, three, four cats hurtle through space, only to have their parachutes fold, I thought how Albert had said his calculations would be perfect and nothing could go wrong. I was glad I hadn't decided to be the parachute tester. I decided I should question everything Albert suggested, or I might not live too long.

Each time one landed, the cat would bound off fast, slowed only by the parachute. Eventually, it would turn on the parachute as the only thing it could take its anger out on. It would rip it to shreds, sending bits of cloth and red baling twine flying in all directions.

Neither of us made a move to grab any more cats nor to get back our parachutes. Instead, we watched each parachute get ripped to shreds, and our parachute testers run off with ribbons of sheet and baling twine following them. I could just imagine the other cats laughing at them. We caught some teasing later from Daniel over the "well-dressed cats in the neighborhood."

Just about the time Albert launched the last cat out, saying, "This one is sure to work," we heard a sound that made our hearts jump.

"Albert, Tommy, where are you? Albeeeeert! Tommyyyyyyyy!"

It was my dad coming through the barn looking for us. He had just stepped out of the back door, and Albert grabbed desperately for the cat he had just let go, but it was too late. We could see the cat descending like a storm cloud toward Dad's head, claws fully extended, like knives drawn and ready for battle. He smacked Dad's head, and, lucky for Dad, he was wearing his milking cap. He still got a few claw marks for good measure. Dad hardly knew what hit him. It reminded me of watching the road runner show. A ten pound furry anvil on the head, knocking him to the ground. Then, in an instant, there was a cat bounding off with a suit of baling twine and sheet.

I turned to Albert to tell him that I thought we better hide, but he was nowhere in sight. Albert, who had kept his wits about him, had disappeared. Dad looked up, and I was sitting alone on the ledge.

Suddenly, I heard Albert's voice from down below by Dad, slightly panting, but in a forced calmness. "Here I am, Dad. I think Tommy is upstairs, but I'm not sure what he's doing."

8

Mighty Hunters

o say that after the cat episode, my backside was sore for about a month is an understatement. My parents often mention that the Bible says, "to spare the rod is to spoil the child," and they do not plan to let me grow up spoiled.

To add insult to it all, Mom came up missing some sheets, and the cats seemed to be wearing them about the farm; pieces of them, anyway. I couldn't convince anyone that I was not the one who took them, nor that Albert had had a hand in it. I had been the one who tried to convince Mom and Dad I needed a cat trap. The pieces all fit together and pointed in my direction.

If I brought up the subject of Albert's involvement, I got a "you wait until we're alone" glare from him, and all Mom and Dad said was, "If that is the case, you should learn not to do everything your brother says."

It was quite a while before I let him talk me into another one of his money making schemes. The next one, however, was to make use of my already-built cat trap.

We have many cottontail rabbits around the farm. These rabbits are cute, but far too pesky. They eat a huge portion of the hay that we store for the farm animals. The cats keep them at bay, but I could never figure out why they never disposed of all of them. Somehow, it just seemed that once someone caught one of these fluffy bundles, it would just lie quietly while it was petted.

We had a pet rabbit for a while. We called him Fluffy. I really loved Fluffy. I used to sit for hours sticking a piece of hay or grass into his pen. He would eat, with his nose wiggling back and forth. I tried to eat that way one day, and my mother told me to go blow my nose.

I saw on a cartoon that rabbits love carrots. I tried to feed Fluffy a carrot, but I found out that he only liked the green tops. Rabbits don't actually eat the orange part. I had a great idea. I went to the garden and cut off about half of my mom's carrot tops. I fed them to Fluffy until he was so round his legs would hardly touch the ground. He looked like a giant cotton ball. I still can't figure out why Mom was so mad. We don't ever eat the tops and never will. Besides, the ones I cut the tops off of must have been done growing because they didn't grow any more after that.

Anyway, Albert got this great idea that if we caught these rabbits, we could make a fortune selling them. At first, he thought we would make fur coats out of them, but we remembered the passing of our sweet Fluffy and decided we would just sell the rabbits in one piece.

You see, one day, Fluffy just came up missing. We looked and looked for him. We assumed he had gotten out of his cage. We called him and called him, but he never came. We just thought it was a coincidence that we had chicken for dinner that night. No one said we were having chicken; they just said we were having meat that tasted like chicken. I was thoroughly enjoying my piece. I even told Mom how good it was.

She coughed a bit then replied, "Why, thank you, dear."

Then Daniel, with his usual impish smile, said, "It sure is funny this **'chicken'** doesn't have any wings."

Mom, in her sternest voice, said, "Daniel!" That was her way of saying, "Don't you start!"

Suddenly, Josie started to cry. Then others began to cry, too. I still didn't understand.

"What is everybody crying about?"

Daniel looked at me and said, "Fluffy sure tastes good, doesn't he?"

Suddenly I felt sick. I couldn't finish my dinner, no matter how long I was threatened with being at the table. Neither could many of my brothers and sisters. Mom ended up having to throw it out, saying we needed to grow up.

Albert and I found rabbit catching wasn't nearly as easy as we had supposed. Rabbits don't fancy getting caught. We chased one around for nearly an hour. The little beggars can squeeze into a hole that a mouse couldn't get through.

With Tippy's help, we flushed one out of a wood pile near the barn. We chased him across the corral at a dead run, dry manure flying at every step. Albert yelled for me to head him off. It is hard to head something off when you are behind it and losing ground. However, Tippy was faster than the rabbit, and turned out to be a great rabbit dog. He bounded across the corral in all his puppy exuberance at racehorse speed, tripping over his huge feet.

Tippy was beginning to show signs of being a mighty hunter, the kind of dog I always dreamed of. I thought, at one point, he was even going to catch the rabbit. But the rabbit took a quick turn, and Tippy went Tippy-over-tea-kettle when he tried to turn. That is the way he usually made a quick turn. But then he was right back after the rabbit. The rabbit ran safely into a hollow log. Tippy, acting like he had treed the most magnificent of animals, let out a howl that sounded like a sick donkey. "Barooooo! Barooooo! Baraooooo!"

The log was from an old barn and was way too heavy for us to lift an end to dump the rabbit out. It was Albert that first had the idea of using the cat trap to catch a cat to flush out the rabbit. I thought that sounded like a great idea because I was proud of my cat trap. Dad made me put it away after the parachute attempts. I think he planned to take an ax to it when I wasn't looking, but I kept an eye on it. It may have been ugly, but it was the first thing I had built that actually worked. I thought it was really something. I think that is the only reason it didn't get thrown on the trash heap; Dad knew how I felt.

Albert and I set up the trap and soon had a cat. It was an orange one and looked a little like a tiger. We quickly put the trap back where it had been stored so no one would wonder what we were up to. We had blocked the ends of the log so that the rabbit couldn't come out, and Tippy stayed at command to work it over if it did.

When we were ready, Albert handed the cat to me.

"You stick the cat in this end, and I will go down to the other end and catch the rabbit when he comes out."

"Why don't *you* put the cat in and let *me* catch the rabbit?"

"Because I am oldest, and I said I would catch the rabbit."

We both took up our positions while Tippy kept running back and forth from end to end. Albert pulled the material out of the log on his end first.

"He's still in there; I can see him about halfway down the log. Go ahead and put the cat in."

"What if the cat tries to come back out my end?"

"Just take out enough stuff to shove the cat in, then close the hole back up."

I took out just enough material that I could barely push the cat through. He started grabbing the gunny sacks we used to stuff up the hole. He also grabbed the log, then he grabbed me, then he grabbed the gunny sack again. I finally got my hand around his front paws so he couldn't grab anything and I stuffed him in again. This time he splayed out his back legs, hooking them onto the log. I held

47

him in place with one hand, pulled the back legs off of the log with the other, and poked him into the hole. I quickly stuffed the gunny sack in to plug it back up.

Albert was down on the ground on his end. He was lying on his side looking into the hole. He had his hands ready to grab the fluffy little cotton tail when it came out. And out it did come.

It hit Albert with all four claws a-blazing. Albert made a valiant grab, and for one brief moment, he had the little fur ball. Then it turned on him with teeth and claw. The claws ripped clear through his shirt and into his chest. His bare arms became a patchwork of scratch lines. Albert fell to his back as the rabbit tore its way to freedom and darted across the barnyard with Tippy hot on its trail.

Albert lay on the ground, panting from shock and pain. I was at the other end of the log, bug-eyed. I had no idea a powder puff rabbit could be so mean. We had a neighbor, Mr. Blanchard, that had a rabbit he claimed ruled the whole farm. He said he would put food in the dog bowl and call for the dog. Mr. Blanchard said that if the dog came first, he would look all around before eating. He said that often, out of nowhere, would come a little white streak, and it would chase the dog clear out to the pasture. Then the little rabbit would come back and eat first, while the dog stood off a good distance with its tail between its legs.

Miguel, a Brazilian farmhand, worked there, and he showed me a scar on his leg that was two thimble-sized round spots about a half inch apart. He told me he had been bitten by the rabbit. He said that when he went to slop the hogs, the rabbit would chase the pigs off until it had a look over the food to see if there was anything it wanted. Mr. Blanchard said he had planned to shoot the rabbit, but it made such a great conversation piece. I never had a run-in with the rabbit myself and thought they were probably telling me a tale. Grownups do that now and then.

But when Albert had the rabbit turn its claws on him, I could see that what people had said could be true. I was very glad Albert had decided to take that end of the log. He sat up half dazed. He was still sitting in front of the open end of the log. I think he was just ready to yell at me when, suddenly, something else hit him. It was orange, black, fur, claws and teeth. We had forgotten that the cat was still in there.

The cat saw a shot at freedom and, even though Albert didn't mean to block its path, the cat had no way of knowing that. The cat jumped on Albert, and Albert threw his arms over his face. The cat did a little dance as it peeled out, then it disappeared.

It would have been funny, except that I had wanted to be on that end of the log. Besides that, Albert was older than me, and he wasn't smiling.

He glared at me. "Whose stupid idea was it to catch the dumb rabbits?"

"It was yours," I answered.

"Don't you get smart with me, or you'll be sorry," he threatened. "I'm not in the mood for it."

9

Where Babies Come From

Dad pulled me onto his lap and told me he had something to tell me. He looked at me very seriously as he spoke. "How would you like to have a new brother or sister?"

"Which one?"

"We don't know yet. Which would you like?"

I thought about this. I figured a brother might be more useful. Albert always made me do his work, and I thought maybe a younger brother would be good to have around. Of course, there was Willie, but it didn't seem like he was ever going to get big enough to help.

On the other hand, a brother would mean sharing the already-crowded bedroom, and I already had to sleep in the same bed as two of my brothers.

"I think I would like to have a sister," I answered. "When will she come?"

"We don't know exactly when the baby will come, and we are not sure it will be a she."

"Then why did you ask?"

This question seemed to perplex Dad.

"I thought you might like to think about it."

"Think about what?"

"Think about having a new baby brother or sister?"

"Why?"

"So you can get ready for it."

I was sure that meant it would be a boy, and he would have to share our bedroom. But I had a more important question to worry about.

"Where do babies come from?" I asked

Dad had a strange look come over his face. He sat there for quite a while, deep in thought, but didn't say anything.

My mom, who had been listening from the kitchen, suddenly spoke. "Well, where do babies come from?"

I was surprised Mom didn't know. After all, I had eight brothers and sisters, and I figured she had probably seen where at least one came from. But maybe Dad had always been the one to get them.

Dad smiled. "Babies come from the hospital."

There was a quick, disgusted snort from Mom in the kitchen. I am not sure she believed him, or maybe she thought it was a bigger deal than that.

Dad continued. "We just go down to the hospital and pick one out."

A loud crash sounded in the kitchen, but Dad went on undisturbed. "They have all sorts of babies there. There are black ones, white ones, brown ones, and yellow ones."

I got excited. "I think I want a black one or a brown one or a yellow one."

Mom snickered, and Dad seemed back to his perplexed face again.

"Well, I think we will stick to white," he stuttered.

Dad had no imagination. He was no fun at all. We already had all white people in our family. Something different would be good for a change, but he seemed stuck on the idea.

"Do you have to spend a lot of money to get a baby at the hospital?" I asked.

"Yes, you do have to spend a lot of money."

"Does a baby cost more than a pony?"

"Yes," he answered.

"Then why don't we just get a pony instead?"

We had a horse I could ride, but she was so big that when I fell off of her, it was like falling off the roof of our house. My friend had a pony, and it was small enough that we didn't get hurt too badly when we fell off. I guess I must have asked Dad too many times for a pony; either that or he was just still determined about the baby idea, even though he could see the pony would save money. Anyway, he suddenly got up and went into the kitchen.

"Is dinner ready yet?" he asked Mom.

Mom didn't answer, but turned to Dad and asked, "We just go to the hospital and pick one out, huh?"

I noticed that Mom was getting bigger. I couldn't sit on her lap because I was clear out on her knee, and I would just fall off. I learned that I needed to be careful mentioning such things. I found out that ladies are very sensitive about it, especially when it is so sudden. Once at church I mentioned that a lady seemed to really be getting big, and Mom scolded me and said it was something we don't say.

It seems it is okay to talk about it if it is a man, but I have never seen a man suddenly get big like that. Mom said that when a lady is pregnant, we say that she is "just glowing." I wasn't sure what pregnant meant, and I was sure the word she meant was "growing" not "glowing." So the next time I saw it happen to a lady, I mentioned that she was just growing, and I got in trouble again.

Grownups can be so strange. Why can't they just use regular words and say what they mean? My mom again told me the word was "glowing," but I still didn't understand. I watched for the lady to come out of the church into the dark evening, and I couldn't see any glowing about her. I figure it must be one of those strange words that has more than one meaning.

Anyway, my mom was glowing so much I couldn't sit on her knee any more when the day came that Mom and Dad told me I was going to visit Grandma.

I love to visit Grandma if the visit isn't too long. If it is long, she always finds a job for me to do, or even worse, she makes me take a nap. This day was one of the long days.

Grandma's house has a long porch that leads to the front door. This old porch has seen better days. It drops on the side away from the house so that it is not level. In the winter, if it is slick, it is hard not to slip and fall.

Just inside the front door is a small foyer that has an old treadle sewing machine and a chest of drawers. The treadle sewing machine is neat. Grandma doesn't use it anymore, but I like to pedal it. I love to hear the whir of the wheel and the che-che-che of the needle going up and down.

There is an old clock on a wooden hutch through an archway. It has little gold balls that spin one way then the other. I like to stand in front of it and twirl my waist way to the left then way to the right then back again.

In the living room there are an old couch and some chairs that Mom and Dad always tell us not to stand on. On the wall behind the couch is a picture that looks like the sun shining through a fog. I like the picture a lot and sometimes stand on the back of the couch to get a better view.

Grandma always has a little candy bowl sitting on the coffee table in the living room. I know better than to help myself, but I also know that if I am good and remember my manners, I might get a piece. It is always the hardtack candy like we get at Christmas, and it is always harder than usual, since it is usually a couple of years old, but candy is candy. I love the red and white striped cherry and mint ones the best.

Of all of the rooms in the house, I love the kitchen most of all. It has old pots and pans hanging from hooks all around the ceiling. It always smells of spices that remind me of Christmas and gingerbread men. It has an old door that leads out onto a back porch and into the back yard.

But Grandma's house also has scary parts. One of them is the cellar. It is entered from the outside. There is a big door that lies on two cement slabs. A person grabs the ring in the door and lifts it up to reveal a stairway.

Mary sometimes reads me stories about things like trolls and goblins that live in strange, dark places. Grandma's cellar is dark, and I'm sure that it must have a hidden door in it that leads into the world of trolls, imps, and fairies. I'm not scared of fairies. They just take your teeth and leave money. But imps and trolls are another story. Only brave knights fight them, and I always feel much braver in the sunlight. It's easier to fight what I can see.

I never go down in the cellar alone, if I can help it. In fact, if I can, I never go down there at all. It is dark and damp and smells moldy and musty. Whenever I step into it, yucky smelling air hits my skin, causing goose bumps to run up and down my back. I'm sure there are monsters in the dark, shadowy corners, waiting to pounce on me if I walk too close.

I was thinking of these things one day when Grandma asked me to step down the stairs and get a bottle of beans. She is getting older, and has a hard time going up and down stairs. I didn't want to, but I knew better than to disobey. I slowly inched my way down the stairs. I kept reminding myself I was not alone; Grandma was at the top of the stairs and would hear my scream if something should reach out a slimy hand and grab me.

I reached out a hand slowly to the quart jar of beans, afraid something might be lurking behind it. Slowly, slowly, I slid my hand around it, ready to dart away at any instant. As my hand closed around it, I jerked it off the shelf and made a mad dash for the stairs and the sunlight above, reaching Grandma in a few bounds.

Grandma frowned. "My, you are acting strange today. Now, go get another one. We need two quarts."

There is only one place nearly as scary as Grandma's cellar, and that is the attic. There are two big bedrooms with beds that stand almost as tall as me. Outside one of the bedrooms is a long hallway that leads to a very steep stairway going downward.

John said that stairway leads to the kitchen and comes out at the one door Grandma always keeps closed, but I'm not sure I believe him. Older brothers exaggerate at times. I often sit in the kitchen and wonder what is behind that door, but it seems too simple to have it just be that stairway. Besides, the stairway is too steep, dark, and scary to simply go to the kitchen.

I thought about trying to open the door to find out, but Grandma keeps her table against it, and I am not strong enough to move the table. I am sure the truth is that the stairs lead down to Grandma's dark cellar to give the trolls and goblins access to the top part of her house.

The beds in the upstairs rooms make me even more sure of this. They are so big that I am positive they belong to some giant or a huge witch or something. And since Grandma never goes upstairs, they just use the upstairs of her house, coming up from the hidden depths of the world of goblins by means of the steep stairs, or flying on a broomstick in through the attic windows.

There is one more thing about Grandma's attic that is the scariest of all. When I climb onto the bed that is in the bedroom nearest the long staircase, I face a big, deep closet. This closet only has a sheet that hangs over it. The sheet always moves back and forth, in and out. John told me it was just because the attic is drafty, but Daniel said that there are monsters living in that closet, and their breathing makes the curtain move in and out. He said it doesn't do any good to hunt for them because they can turn themselves invisible. I'm not about to move the curtain to hunt for them anyway.

My parents left me with Grandma for the whole day. When I had finished lunch, and Grandma announced that I would need to take a nap, I remembered the scary closet and stairway, and I didn't want to.

"But aren't Mom and Dad coming to get me? They almost never leave me here for nap time."

"Well, today they needed to, so you have to take a nap."

"But I don't want to take a nap."

"I didn't ask."

Grandma told me to go upstairs and get in bed. But halfway up the stairs to the attic, there is a landing with a stained glass window. I love to stare out that window, not only because of the rainbow of colors, but because looking at the world outside is like looking through Albert's kaleidoscope. I could see the same picture in many angles. So, of course, I had to stop at the landing and spend some time looking out the window.

"Aren't you up to bed, yet?" Grandma hollered from the bottom of the stairs.

"I was just looking out this pretty window."

"Well, it is time to go to bed."

"I don't want to go to bed. It's scary up there."

"Nonsense! You get to bed this instant."

At that point, I did something no one ever did. I told Grandma no. I knew better, but I was so scared I said it anyway.

Grandma went and got a leather strap.

"You are not going to speak that way to me, young man. Are you going to get into bed, or do I have to use this?"

I decided that maybe Grandma just wanted to feed me to the monsters upstairs, and that made me more determined that I was not going to take a nap.

"I am not going to bed. Grandmas shouldn't be mean and make kids go to bed."

That was it. I was in big trouble. Grandma grabbed me, and gave me a few strong whacks with the leather strap, but I wiggled free and ran past her down the stairs and hid behind the sofa. This slowed her down for a minute, but I couldn't get all of me behind it, and she grabbed my foot and pulled me out.

We got halfway up the stairs with a few more whacks of the strap and, again, I made a desperate dash and found a hiding place. When she finally found me this time, the sweat was pouring off her forehead, and we settled down to talk.

"Why don't you want to go up to bed?"

"Because it's scary up there."

"Fiddlesticks. There is nothing up there but a couple of old beds."

I had always had a lot of faith in Grandma, so I began to feel braver. She added more to sweeten the deal.

"You go up to bed, and your daddy will be here when you wake up. When he comes, he is going to have a big surprise!"

That was enough. With Grandma's assurance of no monsters, and the thought of a reward, I marched up to bed. I doubted just for a minute when I poked my head into the room. Grandma's old beds have real feather that stick out of them. On damp spring days it always smells like our chicken building. I could also see the curtain on the closet moving in and out. But then I thought of Grandma's promise and envisioned a big lollipop. They are my favorite. I can suck on them for hours, and when I get to the middle, I chew the Tootsie roll center. Sometimes Albert asks me for a lick, but he always bites it and takes half of my Tootsie roll.

But he wouldn't get any of this one. If I was going to sleep in the bed at Grandma's, he wasn't going to get a smell, let alone a lick. I opened the door wide enough for me to get in, took a deep breath, and then made a mad dash for the bed. I was sure that if I could get under the big, thick covers, I would be safe. I hit the bed at full speed. I grabbed the covers, tearing my way up the side, and dove under the blankets. I pulled them up over my head, and I was safe.

But then I had another problem -- I was running out of air. I worked a small tunnel into the outside world. It was just big enough that I could look through it and see the curtain moving back and forth and it gave me just enough air to breathe. I figured that as long as the sheet was moving, the monster was still in there, and hadn't turned invisible and snuck into the room. I tried to change my thoughts to lollipops. I began to feel quite warm and safe and very, very tired.

Suddenly, I heard a loud voice from downstairs. It was my dad.

"Tommy! Tommy, wake up! Come down here!"

I forgot all about the monsters and big beds and steep, dark stairways and could only think of lollipops and peppermint candy. It took only a second to unravel myself from the blankets and rush downstairs to my dad.

"Did you bring me a surprise?! Did ya?! Did ya?!"

Dad laughed. "Sure did. Check in the car with your mother."

I rushed out the door, across the tilting porch, and down the rickety front stairs, right over to the old red Rambler.

I jerked the door open. "Where is it, Mom? Where is it? Where is my surprise?"

Mom had a strange quiet smile. "Right here." She pulled back a blanket. "You've got a new baby sister."

What a blow! I had been expecting a lollipop. I had slept in the huge, smelly bed. I had gathered up all that courage to face those monsters, and all I got was a sister! Boy, was I mad. I gathered up all the disgust I could, stood as tall as possible, and said, "Is that all?"

I guess I must have said the wrong thing, because Mom gave me a little whack and sniffled. Grandma came out with Dad and goo-gooed at the baby. I glared at Grandma. Boy, did I feel tricked. Grandma hadn't even offered me a piece of candy out of her candy bowl. I climbed in the back seat and knit my eye brows together. I wanted them to know I was mad. It didn't matter, though. No one paid any attention to me. They only noticed the baby. Pretty soon, my head hurt from keeping my eyebrows knit together, so I had to give it up.

When we got home, everyone had to ooh and aah all over. It all made me madder and madder. Finally, someone turned and asked if I wanted to hold her.

"No! I don't want her!"

"Oh," someone said, "I think he's jealous."

I wasn't jealous. She was pink and wrinkled and she smelled funny. Why would I want to be pink and wrinkled and smell funny? And to make matters worse, we got her instead of a lollipop. Why did they think, after all of that, I was suppose to ooh and aah all over her? Ha! Fat chance. Not me.

But the next thing I knew, I was lifted onto the couch and she was stuck on my lap. I put my hand up by her face, and she immediately turned and tried to suck on it. I thought that was funny. I put my hand by the other side, and she turned the other way. It was a neat game. I could just put my hand on one side, and then the other, and she would turn her head that way. It was great fun, until somebody decided I was teasing her and took her away.

I don't get it. They want me to like her, and when I start having fun with her, they take her away.

John asked Dad how much the hospital bill was.

"Well, we haven't gotten it yet, but I assume it will be around eight hundred dollars."

I don't know exactly how much eight hundred dollars is, but I know it must be a lot. A few mornings later, when Dad came out of his room all sleepy eyed, and announced that he hadn't gotten much sleep because the baby had cried all night, I didn't feel one bit sorry for him.

"Why don't you take her back to the hospital and get your money back?" I asked. "I bet you could get a lot of lollipops for eight hundred dollars."

10

Sunday School

Sunday School isn't too bad, except for one thing. Actually, come to think of it, Sunday School is that bad. The sun is shining outside, and I get stuck in a stupid classroom. Tippy is lucky because he doesn't have to go to Sunday School. I wish I could be a dog.

Since we live a few miles out of town on a dairy farm, I almost never see other five- and six-year-olds, except at church meetings, and then, most of the day, we are stuck in church.

It happened that on this morning I again found myself sitting on a hard bench, and the only thing I could do is wonder why class wasn't over yet. It was a beautiful summer day, and I just wanted to be outside.

I seemed to always be getting into trouble, too. Most of the girls that sit in front of me come to church with neatly braided hair. When it is in two strands, it looks like the two ropes of the bridle we use on our horse. I love to grab those two strands, one in each hand, and whip them up and down, yelling, "Yah! Yah! Get up there. Yah! Yah!" The girls don't seem to appreciate it, though, and neither does the teacher.

If it is one thicker strand down the girl's back, it looks like the big rope we swing on in Uncle Darren's barn. Sometimes my cousins and I try to climb that rope and see if we can get up to the top and reach the beam. I can never reach the beam. I usually only get barely off of the ground.

But there I was this morning in Sunday School, and I couldn't believe class wasn't over yet. The teacher was telling us stories of Bible heroes. I actually like Bible stories. My sister, Mary, reads them to me all of the time out of the Bible reader, and I know them all by heart. But the stories in the Bible reader are exciting. Our teacher isn't exciting at all.

"... and Moses climbed the mountain to see the burning bush..."

That's it! I would climb the rope to the top of the world's highest mountain. Hand over hand I went until I reached the girl's head, which, of course, was not really a girl's head, but the craggy ridge of the rock ledge at the top of the world's highest mountain. Then, with one huge effort, I would pull myself up over the ledge to plant the flag of my country on the summit no one had ever been on before.

There was one problem, however. The girl didn't hold her head steady. Instead, as I gave my last great effort, her head popped back against the bench. Rather than making it up over the edge, the ledge suddenly gave way before me. As I scrambled to get away from the deadly rock slide, I reached up over the ledge and the falling rock, grabbing onto the nose, or chin, or whatever other rock I could get hold of.

I also had to pull harder and harder on the rope as the rocks tumbled by me into the gully below. Right then the girl raised her hand. The teacher, cut off in mid sentence, glared down her nose at me. My whole hand covered the girl's face, and the girl was making muffled gagging noises.

"And as Daniel was thrown into the lions' ... Tommy, what are you doing?"

"Um. .... I am climbing out of the lions' den."

"You were doing no such thing. You were pulling Joanne's hair, now, weren't you?"

I suppose to the ordinary, untrained eye, that was probably what it looked like. There wasn't any reason to argue because my Sunday School teacher isn't a mountain climber.

She does look like she might have been a sumo wrestler at some time in her life. She isn't the kind of lady a person wants to mess with. She is roughly the size of a giant gorilla, and she reads her lesson with her glasses on. When she wants to see someone, she pulls them down to the end of her nose and glares over them.

"You march yourself right up here this instant, young man," she commanded.

I always hate this part. I figure it's Joanne's fault anyway. If she doesn't want her pigtail pulled, she shouldn't wear one. But I knew no matter what I said, I was in trouble. Even if it is Sunday School, and the teacher talks on and on about mercy, all she really wants is justice.

"You march right down the hall and find your mother," she ordered.

I hoped that if I took my time going down the hallway, class would be over by the time I got to the room my mother was in. I obediently headed down the hall, but since the teacher said march, I decided I would be a wind-up toy soldier. I swung my foot slowly around, and then brought the heel of it back against the toe of my other foot. Then I brought the other foot slowly around and brought the heel back against the toe of the first foot. Covering that distance was painfully slow that way.

However, I found myself getting close to the door of the room my mother was in, and class time was still far from over. Just then, I found my toy soldier spring running down, and I came to a complete halt. My body just went limp and stopped.

At that moment, my teacher, who had been watching the whole thing out of the doorway, snuck up behind me and scared me to death. "Get movin'!" That wound up my spring again.

I stepped into the adult class, and all eyes turned to me. The teacher looked me over and said, "Proverbs tells us, 'a child left to himself bringeth his mother to shame.' "

I think he made that up.

Mom wasn't about to leave me to myself. She asked me why I was sent to her.

"I don't think the teacher likes me." I said. I figured that was a true statement.

"And why doesn't she like you?" she asked.

That stumped me. Tippy likes me, and he's a dog. He doesn't mind if I climb over the bench. He doesn't mind if I climb anything. In fact, he likes to climb them with me. Then it hit me. Maybe she is jealous because I can climb under the bench, while she has to stand up there and teach. I didn't know how to say all of that, so I just said something my dad said once about a lady that was upset.

"Maybe her pantyhose are too tight."

The ladies sitting next to my mother gasped. I wondered if perhaps their pantyhose were too tight, too.

The old man sitting beside them laughed. "Don't get your dander up," he said. "I bet he's probably right." Then he laughed all over again.

Mom wasn't laughing. She took me out into the hall. She looked me straight in the eye and said, "Your teacher doesn't hate you. She just doesn't appreciate misbehavior. Now, what were you doing to make her mad?"

I told her I was just showing the class the proper method for Daniel to climb out of the lions' den.

"And just how is that?"

I knew that if I told her I was using Joanne's hair, she would get mad. I also knew that if I didn't tell her, she would probably hear it from Joanne's mother. I also knew that if a person tells a lie in church, a brick is likely to break loose and fall on his head. So I told the truth in the simplest way I could. "Joanne helped me."

I think Mom figured she wasn't getting anywhere, because she let out an exasperated sigh, told me off, and said I "better behave, or else." I have never figured out what the "or else" is, but I know by the way she says it that I never want to find out. She then walked with me back to class, afraid I might get lost or something.

I could hardly believe class wasn't over yet. The teacher was still telling us about great Old Testament heroes.

"Elijah hid in a cave for many days and was fed by ravens," she droned.

That was no big deal for a great cave explorer like myself. The shadow of the bench in front of me made a great cave to explore. Once down on my hands and knees, I noticed that the tiles on the floor were probably dinosaur bones waiting to be dug up.

I figured a bear even lived in this cave. Why, there were even some bear droppings there. Either that or somebody stepped in some dog doo out on the lawn.

And ravens. Who is scared of a raven? I had uglier things than ravens. There were bats in my cave. Most of them had beady little eyes. I could see lots of them peeping out from Lori's shoes, each pair of eyelets glowing silver in the dark shadows.

I didn't want to get too deep into this cave and not be able to find my way out. I had heard stories of great cave explorers that would tie strings together so they would have something to follow back out of the cave. That sounded like a smart idea.

Of course, the only things available to me in my cave were shoe laces, but there were lots of them. I quietly undid each shoelace, so I wouldn't waken any sleeping bears, and then I tied them all together. I had to tie one to the bench at the mouth of the cave. I wanted that end to stay put.

"...And, as David approached Goliath,... Tommy, what are you doing under that bench?"

"Uh, I am exploring Elijah's cave to make sure there are no bears."

"You are doing no such thing. You get out from under there. You can see the girls are wearing dresses, and a little boy shouldn't be under their bench."

"Then can I play under the boys' bench?"

"You most certainly cannot. Gentlemen do not crawl under benches. You get right up and sit down this instant."

I don't know what a gentleman is, but it sounds very boring, and I'm sure I don't want to be one. However, I knew better then to disobey. At least I wasn't marching down to my mother.

Of course, Carolyn had to turn around and smirk her, "You got in trouble again, Smarty" smirk. She is about 10 months older than the rest of us, and she has a gap in her teeth wide enough to drive a herd of sheep through. With her red hair she looks like a jack-o-lantern.

I could hardly believe this class wasn't over yet. Instead, the teacher continued on.

"As I was saying before I was so rudely interrupted, David showed great courage in standing up to Goliath. He approached swinging a simple sling with a rock against this mighty warrior. Goliath just laughed at him..."

Goliath wouldn't have laughed at me had I been David. Granted, I don't have a sling, but I am a deadly aim with a rubber band. That reminded me that I had brought one with me.

It wasn't one of those simple little skinny kinds, either. Oh, no. I was much too strong for those. It was one of the big, super thick ones. I had saved a church bulletin for just this purpose. I broke off little pieces of paper and folded them into triangles.

Suzanne had long black hair that fell loose past her shoulders. It looked like the beard of an enemy. The two hair pins on the sides looked like long, slitted eyes just glaring out from the hairy face. I could even smell the stench of his breath - a stench so powerful that he must have drunk a whole bottle of hair spray.

Laugh at me, would he? I sneered at the ugly face and fired my first shot. The thickness of the mass of hair blocked penetration to the vital forehead that I knew I had to reach before I could drop this ugly giant. Again and again I fired, but the deadly foe seemed unfazed.

I had to resort to more deadly weapons. After folding the paper into triangles, I spit on them to add to their potency. Again and again I fired, but still the ugly face just glared back at me. Although he was now marked up with the paper fragments, the giant was still unfazed.

"Then there was Gideon."

Twang.

"Gideon was a man of great..."

Twang.

"As I was saying, Gideon ..."

Twang.

"Tommy, what in the world are you doing now?!"

I could hear the exasperation in my teacher's voice.

"I am trying to take care of Goliath," I answered.

"You are not. You're flippin' a rubber band. Give it to me."

"But it's mine," I protested.

"Correction," she said. "It **WAS** yours. Now it's mine."

I couldn't believe this class wasn't over yet.

The teacher grabbed my rubber band and pulled. Talk about a lousy Sunday School class when the teacher steals your rubber band. I held on with all of my might, but the teacher was a lot stronger than I was. As the rubber band stretched out to about as long as I am tall, and my fingers felt like they would fall off, I had to let go.

Pop! It shot free at a tremendous speed. It caught the teacher across the face, leaving a nasty, huge, red welt. She lost her balance and sprawled flat on the floor in her dress. When she looked up, I could see the desire to kill something in her eyes, and I knew that something was me. She scrambled to her feet, ruffled but determined, as she mumbled something about "spare the rod and spoil the doggone child," and she reached for the yardstick.

I really, **REALLY** couldn't believe class wasn't over yet.

As she turned back to face the class, she stepped up in front of the girls' bench and, just as she was going to reach over and teach me something about the staff of Moses, the bell rang, and I knew there was a God, and that he does answer prayers!

I ran for the door as fast as I could. The teacher jumped up close to the girls' bench to get into good batting position. The girls screamed and, trying to get out of the path of the swinging yardstick, made a break for the door. Unfortunately, I had never finished my cave exploration, and all of the shoelaces were still tied together and roped to the end of the bench at the cave opening. As the teacher took a swing and the girls headed for the door, there was suddenly a mass of petticoats, arms, legs, and a yardstick.

...And thus it was that, because Gideon trusted in the Lord, the Midionites, in their great confusion, fell upon their own yardsticks and were destroyed.

11

The Witch's House

etting out after Sunday School on a summer day is like a release from a life sentence. We meet in a little green country church. It has green and brown lawns all around with a little green building in the back. There is a sheep net fence that borders the church property that has a log rail on the top. The fence goes around a field that is used as a church ball diamond, rodeo ground, carnival center, and a cow pasture when it isn't otherwise occupied. The last makes it so there is no need to mow or fertilize it.

That is okay, except that during the baseball games, the players have to dodge cow pies here and there. Sometimes cow pies make convenient bases, but everyone is always being accused of not touching the bases and, when they aren't dry, it makes everyone think twice about sliding.

Almost everyone at church is a descendant of the pioneers that settled our valley. We hear stories about them all of the time. Almost everyone farms, too. My dad said the farmers are the salt of the earth because they are a hardworking, God-fearing people. I don't know what it means to be the salt of the earth, but I know that almost everyone has tough, brown skin from many years of work in the baking sun and freezing cold, so I think it has something to do with that.

All of us boys like to brag about how tough we are. The hours of changing pipe, hauling hay, and working with cattle make us that way. Even at my age, my dad feels I should be able to roll bales into line, haul straw, and help in many other ways. Except for church, I look forward to Sunday. Dad says it is the Lord's Day, so the only work we have to do is to milk the cows and feed the animals.

When church gets out, I love to go outside and play. I don't get to see other children very often, so it's my big chance. I especially like to play tackle football, using a hymn book for the ball. Wrestling is also fun. I can beat any boy my age or even a year older. But I almost always come home with grass stains on my suit.

My mom isn't happy about that, even when I get my suits from hand-me-downs or the second hand store. She was especially upset the day I came home with grass stains on my new navy blue suit. She made it sound like I had committed some unpardonable sin. I may have had grass stains on my pants, and my shirt might have been ripped, but I didn't have a mark on my tie or my suit coat. In fact, I couldn't even find them. Those had come off the minute I stepped out the door, and who knows where they went?

My mom tells me off week after week about the grass stains. It doesn't do any good. After escaping from a Sunday School classroom, I can't help it, especially in the springtime after a long cold winter.

Mom ended up buying me a new suit that is green - grass green. I hate the color, but every week, after Mom sponges it off, a person can barely see any grass stains on it.

I figure it isn't my fault. It is no different than the cows we keep locked up in the barn all winter. As the smell of spring and fresh grass start to flow across the breeze, the cows begin to grow restless. I was excited the day my dad told me that he thought the pastures had dried out enough that the cows could be turned out to graze. I threw open the barn doors and watched the cows gallop across the barn yard. I do have a bit of a mean streak in me, though. I had gone and shut the corral gate first. The cows took off, only to find their access to the lush pastures blocked. Then I stood at the gate and let them through a few at a time.

"Oh, so sorry Bossy, you kicked me yesterday. I am afraid you are going to have to be last." I kept the ornery ones back until, finally, like a bottle of fermenting grass and sour milk, they charged, Bossy at the front.

Anyway, getting out of church is like that. The freedom, I mean. A person can run and let the fresh spring air swirl about us.

Across the parking lot are some wonderful bushes. There are some with white berries that ooze out a gooey white liquid when we smash them. Of course, to truly have fun, a person has to have someone to smash them on.

This, of course, is what girls are good for. The boys' favorite target is Suzanne. This is not just because she has the prettiest black hair, so that when a big handful of berries is smashed in it she looks like a skunk with a drippy stripe.

Nor is it because she has the sweetest temperament of the girls and won't slap a person silly like Caroline will. These are all true. But the biggest reason is because she is the prettiest, and all of us boys like her.

A person might ask, why we do it at all if we like her? That is a dumb question. The answer is fairly obvious. It is because,... well, it's just because. That's what boys do, that's why.

When the berries come on, church is at its best -- after church, anyway. We form into two teams with rubber bands, that is, if the teacher hasn't taken them, and we use the bushes for forts. We fire the berries at each other. A sideswipe is a point, a direct hit is five points, a hit in the face is twenty-five, and one in the mouth, well, one in the mouth is too good to beat, so a person might as well call the game and declare the winner.

There is only one plant that can beat the white berries, and that is the spear weed. I don't know what its real name is, but we call it the spear weed. We call it that because it has little grass pockets, and tucked into each one is a small grass spear. We can pull this out and throw it. The spear handle is just longer than my dad's hand, just the right size to get a good grip on. Each spear will give just a little pin prick, but will stay attached to the victim. You can tell which girls we like the most because they have lots of spears sticking out of them. Suzanne always goes home looking like a porcupine.

We also like to play Israelites and Philistines. We form our armies and get our spears. Scriptures make good shields. At least they did until our mothers told us that it was sacrilegious. I'm not sure what sacrilegious means, but I think it has something to do with how expensive something is. Anyway, they made us stop using them, and we now have to use our suit coats instead.

That's what we were doing the day Frank Angstrom came to us. His dad is one of the leaders of the congregation. Frank asked us if we wanted to see something. He was about nine years older than us, and big, so, of course, we were interested. We were too scared of him not to be. He took us all around behind the church to the area where we almost never went. There is a small green building there, the same color as the church. He showed us all around it. Its roof was falling in, and some of the bricks were crumbling.

"Do you know what this is?" he asked with an air of great wisdom. "It is the doorway to a witch's underground chamber."

He really had our attention now. The ugly old building looked as if his story were true. There was a door that looked to be about a foot thick, and had a big padlock on it.

"Do you know why the door is always locked?" he continued.

We told him we didn't. I wasn't sure I even wanted to know.

He continued on in a scary voice. "Many years ago, the witch would sneak out and catch small boys who weren't being careful and cook them up for her dinner. Then, one Sunday night, as the moon was full and rising high in the sky, the men of the church caught her. After the men caught her, they built this house over the opening to her chamber and locked the door. Sometimes, if you listen carefully, you can hear her. She turns herself into a wolf and howls to be released.

"I have borrowed my dad's keys, and thought you guys might like to see the witch."

I was sure I didn't want to, but I didn't want to act afraid. I was too scared to run away anyway.

He unlocked the lock off the door and turned the knob, then he stopped, and turned to us.

"Oh. I forgot. In order to see the witch, someone will have to be sacrificed to be her meal. Who's it going to be?"

Next to me, I heard a whimper, and I turned to see a yellow streak beginning to form down the leg of Butch's nice, new, cream-colored suit. I was grateful my suit was dark green.

Frank eyed up and down the row of us shivering boys, and said, "Surely, one of you brave boys would like to volunteer. We'll just open the door enough to toss you inside and let her eat her fill of you."

Just as he said that, a horrible squealing and groaning sound started coming out from inside.

"Oh, no!" Frank yelled. "She's heard us! We've got to feed her quickly!" We were unaware that his friends had snuck up behind us, and Frank yelled, "Grab them, guys!" We turned to see three thirteen and fourteen-year-old boys bearing down on us. We ran, but they caught us and brought us back to the door of the witch's underground cavern.

"Well, well, well," Frank said. "I think we have enough here to feed the witch for a year."

We were all screaming for help as loud as we could when Frank covered my mouth. "Quiet now! You wouldn't want to make the witch mad."

That quieted us, except for Butch, who continued to whimper. I looked over at him and could see that most of the front of his suit pants were yellow now.

Frank looked at us. "None of you guys seem to want to see the witch."

We assured him we didn't. "Well," he said, "we definitely need something to feed to her. What are we going to do?"

Buster suggested we could feed her Twinkies. Frank said, "You know, I think that might work. Are you going to bring her some?" Buster said he could bring some when he came to the evening meeting at 7:00. "See that you do," Frank said, and they let him go.

Butch thought the witch might like Ding-Dongs, and Frank agreed. Then it was my turn. My head was reeling. I said I thought the witch might like oatmeal cookies. My mom had just made some the day before.

Frank gave me a narrow stare, "Do they have raisins? The witch doesn't like raisins." I couldn't remember if they had raisins or not, but I assured him they wouldn't. The older boys let me go, and, as I ran for the front of the church, I could hear them calling a reminder for me to bring them "tonight." They said they would be waiting by the edge of the "dark side" of the church.

I was relieved to be safely in our car and heading home for dinner instead of **being** dinner. My cousins that live in the city have their main meal in the evening. They call it dinner and call the one at noon lunch. But we have our main dinner meal at noon, so we call that dinner and call the evening meal supper.

Sunday dinner is the best. Every week Mom puts a pot roast in the oven, flavored with carrots and onions around the side. Baked potatoes are set in the oven to cook, too. While we change our clothes, Mom takes the drippings of the roast and makes up a dark gravy. She always cooks corn or peas to go with it.

The roast is always browned with a slight crisp edge. The potatoes are golden with a crunchy shell. I love to dig the soft inside out of the potatoes and mash it, then pour the rich, dark gravy over the pile, with a little extra running off to dip my meat in. I take the crisp, brown shell of the potato and put butter and salt inside, then squeeze the shell until the butter runs out. Then I take a bite. The creamy salt and potato flavor melts in my mouth and runs down my throat. We always have plenty of cold milk or icy lemonade to drink.

For supper on Sunday, after a big meal for dinner at noon, my mother doesn't like to cook, so we usually have tuna fish sandwiches. We almost always have green punch to go with them.

We are each allowed two oatmeal cookies for dessert. I hoped to sneak more, but I quickly realized that there were barely enough to go around. I got my two cookies and a plastic bag and went to my room. As I looked at the cookies, I realized with great horror that they had raisins. I love raisins, but Frank said the witch didn't.

I would have to take out all of the raisins. It took a long time, but eventually I had eaten all of the raisins and stood there with a bag full of crumbs. That is not how I expected it to turn out, and I wasn't sure the witch would appreciate it, but the raisins wouldn't come out any other way.

Then I had another idea. My mother makes wonderful homemade bread. I thought perhaps I could take some of that. I knew the only way I could sneak it out was to put it in my suit coat. My mother was surprised when I got dressed early and came out into the kitchen.

She cut me a slice of bread. "Do you want butter on it?"

If it were for me, I would have, but I could just see stuffing it in my coat pocket and having butter drip through. I thought I better play it safe. "No," I said.

"No, what?" my mother corrected me.

"No, thank you," I answered.

I waited until no one was looking and quickly stuffed the bread into my pocket. It didn't fit nicely, so I had to fold it once both directions. I did this very carefully so it would be nice. I waited long enough to not draw attention, then I asked for another piece.

"You ate the first one already?" my mother asked.

I really didn't want to lie, especially before going to church, so I told an off-the-subject truth. "I was hungry," I said.

"Well," my mother informed me, "I think you need to learn to eat slower. Wolfing something down like that could give you indigestion." She then went on extolling the virtues of tasting food and questioning why she should take so long to cook it if we just ate it and never tasted it. But, finally, I got another piece. This one was mine. Witch or no witch, I was hungry, too.

I ate it and wanted another, but I was afraid asking would raise suspicion. I got what other food I could, then got a big drink of water.

When we arrived at church, I sat on the end of the bench. I always like to sit there so I can look around the edge and see the older boys in the back. Tonight, however, I didn't dare look in case Frank was there.

Church had just started when Mrs. Angstrom came in. She came up to our bench, and our family dutifully scooted down. I hated this. She was going to get the best seat, the one on the end of the bench. I have always felt this is so unfair. People who come late to church get the best seats. If it had been my church, I would have made them sit in the middle on the front row, but instead, they get to push everyone over and take the end.

I decided I would ignore her, and maybe she would go away. When everyone else scooted down, she just assumed I would, too. I had turned my head to ignore her, and she didn't look where she was sitting and sat right on me. I am not just talking on my lap. An elephant cannot sit on the lap of an ant. I was pretty well mashed into the bench. I thought I was going to die from suffocation. My dad reached over and tried to pull me out from under her. It was no good. I couldn't move. I thought he was going to pull my arm off. Finally, she stood up enough that my dad could pull me over. I imagined I looked flat, like one of Mary's paper dolls.

My dad didn't get me over far enough before she sat down again. She sat half on my leg and pinched the skin against the bench. I tried to scream, but I still couldn't breathe. I wriggled until my skin popped out from under her, but now I was squeezed between her and my dad, unable to move. Man, I hate church!

I didn't think church would ever end. I wasn't anxious to meet Frank and his friends, but I decided being eaten by a witch was preferable to being squashed by a buffalo. Finally, church did end, and the moment of truth arrived.

Although I tried to stay in areas by the adults, one of Frank's friends eventually caught me and dragged me back to the witch's house. Butch and Buster were already there.

"Well, let's see what you brought her," Frank demanded.

Buster pulled out a Twinkie. The package was supposed to have two in it, but there was only one.

"Where's the other Twinkie?" Frank asked. "One Twinkie will only make her hungrier."

"Uh, well, uh, church went so long, and I...," stammered Buster, as Twinkie crumbs fell from his face.

Frank glared. "You ate the witch's Twinkie? Boy, is she going to be mad."

"But it was my Twinkie," Buster complained. "I just brought it for her."

"No problem," Frank said. "Twinkies make you fat, and the witch loves fat boys."

Buster whimpered. "We'll give you one more chance," Frank said, "but you need to do better next week."

They let Buster go. Next, it was Butch's turn. "Well?" Frank asked. Butch, the always Mr. Smart, had cut open the Ding-Dongs and eaten out the cream filling. His bag contained only the outer cake part.

"What did you do to my... I mean, the witch's Ding-Dong?" Frank demanded.

"I ate the cream filling," Butch said.

"I can see you ate the cream filling!" Frank exclaimed. "What I want to know is why!"

"Well, I thought a witch probably wouldn't like the cream filling," Butch said.

"Well, you thought wrong!" Frank hollered.

I looked over at Butch and could see the whole front of his pants was almost instantly yellow.

"We better hang onto him for a minute while we decide what to do," Frank growled.

I was brought up next. Frank looked me over. "I hope you can do better than the other two."

I pulled the bag of cookie crumbs from my pocket.

Frank was skeptical "But it's just crumbs."

"I took out the raisins," I told him.

Frank scowled. "You took out the raisins and brought us a bunch of crumbs? That will impress the witch."

"But I also brought some homemade bread," I quickly added.

Frank nodded. "Homemade bread would be good."

I pulled the bread out of my pocket, but to my horror it was smashed flat. In the unfortunate crushing I had received on the church pew, when I got steam rolled by Mrs. Giant Woman, it had been mashed into a doughy ball, and it looked terrible.

"This is the best you can do?" Frank asked.

"I had to give up part of my dinner for this," I replied.

"Oh, our hearts are bleeding for you," Frank scoffed.

"Well, I'm not afraid of any old witch," I answered bravely, "and I think you're just a big jerk."

Frank's face flushed red. "Oh, yeah? Well, then, you can be the first to meet the witch. Bring him forward!"

As the boy holding me brought me toward the door, I slammed my foot down hard on his and, with all of my strength, I kicked him in the shin. His grip loosened just enough so that I could jerk free. I took off as fast as I could run, and I heard Frank yell, "Get him!"

I figured that if I could just get to the front of the church, I could probably get in among the grownups and be safe. But just as I came around the first corner, I ran into someone, or something, and Frank and the guy who'd been holding me plowed into my back.

I looked up, and I saw a silhouette against the moon that I knew had to be a werewolf. I froze, unable to run further. The werewolf's voice boomed out. "Frank, what's going on here?"

"Uh, nothing, Dad," Frank said quietly.

"He was planning on feeding us to the witch," I said.

"The witch?" Mr. Angstrom asked. "What witch?"

"The one that lives in the little green building behind the church," I answered.

Mr. Angstrom stood there quietly for a minute. When he finally spoke, it was Frank who was trembling.

"Frank, do you have my keys again?"

Frank pulled out the keys and sheepishly handed them to his dad. "Now, get home," Mr. Angstrom roared. "I'll deal with you later." As Frank ran off, Mr. Angstrom turned to the guy who had been holding me. "You get home, too, young Dalton, or I will have a word with your father."

The boy scampered off as fast as he could. Then, turning to me, he kindly said, "Now, about that witch. I want to show you something."

I didn't actually think I wanted to see anything at this point, but I didn't want to be the one to tell him.

"Come with me," Mr. Angstrom said, and led the way back toward the witch's house. I wanted to go the other way, but if Mrs. Angstrom was big, Mr. Angstrom was bigger, so I followed.

When we got to the witch's house, I was trembling. I didn't think Mr. Angstrom would feed me to the witch, so I tried to be brave.

"Sometimes in life," Mr. Angstrom said, "we have nothing to fear but fear itself. The fear of things unknown is one of our greatest terrors, and yet, the unknown often brings us the greatest opportunities. If we don't take the opportunity to reach out into the unknown, we often just stay in the same old rut we are always in. One thing that will help us to overcome our fear and thus reach out into the unknown and more opportunities is knowledge. Once a person has knowledge, he no longer needs to fear."

I didn't have a clue as to what he was talking about, but I did know that, by this time, he had reached the door and was unlocking it. I expected a witch to jump out at any moment. But I also knew that Mr. Angstrom was in front of me, and that the witch would have to go through him first. I stood there, ready to run.

Just as he was getting the lock undone, the most hideous squealing and screeching noise started up, the same sound we'd heard earlier. I thought to myself, "he woke her up, and she's mad," but he wasn't even ruffled. I wanted to run, but I couldn't make my legs move.

He swung the door open wide, and as he did, it made the most horrible, gravelly, groaning sound. He then reached in and pulled a string, and suddenly, the night was filled with light. I couldn't see for just an instant because it was so bright. When I finally could see, what I saw was not a witch, but a huge wheel turning around. As it turned, it raised a lever up and down. Behind it was a big tank.

"This," Mr. Angstrom explained, "is the pump house. This machine is the pump that brings water into the church. The pump puts water into the tank, but it only turns on when it needs to pressurize the tank."

It was one of the coolest machines I had ever seen. As it sat there cranking away, I was amazed at its sound and motion. Eventually it came to a halt, just as suddenly as it had started.

"Remember," he said, as he shut off the light and closed the door, "there is nothing you need to fear but fear itself. Now that you know what is actually there, you no longer need to be afraid."

As I walked around the church, I felt a new confidence. When I reached the front, Butch and Buster came out from hiding in the bushes.

Butch came running up to me. "What happened to you?"

"I met the witch," I said, acting really important. "And you don't need to worry. You can bring your Twinkies and Ding-Dongs to me, and I'll feed her for you."

12

Fourth Of July

It was the Fourth of July. I'm sure to most people that means fireworks, parades, and many other fun things for celebration. For my family, it usually just means another day of hauling hay. When it is haying season, nothing gets in the way. We have to get the hay in before the rain comes, or it will rot.

My job is to roll bales into straight rows so they can run up the piler to the truck for my brothers to stack. The sun is always hot, and the sweat rolls down my face and stings my eyes. I hate hauling hay almost as much as I hate milking.

But this Fourth of July was different. It had been raining all week, and that meant the hay was too wet to haul. To add to that, my aunt, uncle, and cousins came up from California. Some of my girl cousins are nice enough, but Blair - he is a Mister Know-It-All.

Anyway, my dad wasn't quite sure what to do. We hadn't ever done any celebrating for the Fourth of July except the church flag raising. We always went to that.

The flag raising is always just after sunrise, which means we have to get up really really early to get our chores done. Even then we still have to hurry fast to get there on time. The older men in the congregation set up gas grills just outside the church doors, next to the old wooden flag pole.

The scouts do the flag ceremony, followed by Daniel playing the trumpet. We sing "The Star Spangled Banner," and then someone who was in a war sometime in the past two hundred years talks for nearly forever. Meanwhile, I can smell pancakes, eggs, hash browns, bacon, and sausage cooking.

And listening to some of the speakers talk, a person would think they won the war by themselves. They talked about The Great War and how they used horses and such things.

I watch images of the Vietnam War on our television, when it works, and I know they don't use horses anymore. But no one likes to talk about the Vietnam War. They only talk of past wars, as if those are the only ones that are important.

Don't get me wrong, I'm not against them talking about such things. I'm as patriotic as the next guy, but the next guy was Buster, and I could hear his stomach growling, and it wasn't playing "America the Beautiful." We truly are patriotic. It's just that our stomachs aren't. Finally, when the speaker finishes and breakfast is announced, we boys make a mad dash to the breakfast table.

Our mothers always call us back, saying, "Girls first." They say they do it to teach us manners, but I think they actually do it to get us to not like the girls, which is easy to do, especially Caroline, who always grins her toothless 'so there' grin at us.

Well, sometime after about the day after tomorrow, we finally get to eat, and there is plenty, and no one ever scolds us for going back for more.

That is the way the Fourth of July goes every year, that and going home to face hauling hay in the heat of the day. At least, that is the way it went until this year.

We got home from the breakfast, and we couldn't haul hay, so my dad wasn't quite sure what to do. He suggested fixing some fence and weeding some potatoes. John offered that we ought to take our cousins to the community celebration. Dad scratched his head. I don't think he had ever considered not working this time of year, but he finally declared it a holiday. We would go to the parade, the community celebration that followed, and then we would go fishing until milking time.

I was excited. This would be my first Fourth of July parade. We always went to the one on July 24th, which was called "Pioneer Days" and celebrated our pioneer heritage. We went to that one because haying was done by July 24th.

The Pioneer Days parade was in St. Anthony, in the south of the county. But the Fourth of July parade was in Ashton, in the north of the county. My dad said the two towns worked that out years ago. That way, no one had to do it all, and everyone in the county could celebrate both.

I like Ashton. It has a main street that is about six blocks long, unless you don't count the grain elevators, which would take away two blocks. There are a couple of little stores that sell handmade furniture. There is one theater, some craft stores, one café, and a bar. That is pretty much the whole of Main Street.

My dad always says that in Ashton, everybody knows everybody, and who they don't know, they are related to. There are no stop lights or crosswalks; Ashton doesn't need them. There isn't that much traffic, and people cross the road anywhere they darn well please, even if there is traffic coming, which there almost never is.

Just off of Main Street there is a little hamburger shop that changes names and owners every couple of years. It is only open from Memorial Day to Labor Day – tourist season. Currently, its name is "The Frost Top." There is also a small R.V. park and a motel with little cabins that I think are built for dwarfs or something because each one is so small. In addition, there is one all-purpose gas-station grocery-store hardware-store. We are not talking Sears; we are talking it only carries one variety of anything, and, if that doesn't do, well, that is just too bad.

The tractor dealership just outside of town sells mostly John Deere tractors, but they can pretty much order anything a person wants.

The main part of town is visible from far away because of the giant granaries near the grain elevator. That is where the scale is where we weigh our hay. We almost always buy our hay in Ashton or Mud Lake, so I am in Ashton a lot. I also have quite a few relatives that live there.

The parade started off with a police car. I don't think this is because it makes it look official, but it is more likely because people were standing in the middle of the street visiting, and the police car was to get them to move to the sidewalks. As it approached where we were, people still didn't move, and the police officer gave his siren a blast. Someone yelled back, "All right, Thompson! Don't get shovey! Don't get shovey!"

Blair let me know that this definitely was no Rose Parade. I don't know what a Rose Parade is, but I do know I don't like him bad-mouthing Ashton.

As the parade went on, people strolled back and forth from one side of the street to the other between the floats. Blair said that it wasn't proper, but my dad said, "A parade is only as good as the number of friends you can meet."

Following the police car, there were the veterans marching with the flags. My dad, himself a veteran of World War II, made sure we showed respect for the flag. I felt very proud standing there with my hand over my heart, even though it was the wrong hand, and my dad had to tell me to switch. The veterans are getting older every year, and every year, the flag seems to droop more at the parades. My dad said that because of the way the Vietnam War is viewed, no younger veterans are joining them.

The marching bands followed the veterans. Actually, there ended up being only one that marched. The other one rode on the back of a semi-truck. I always love the marching bands in their sharp uniforms carrying their shiny brass instruments. And I could almost make out what tune they were playing.

The girls' drill teams followed the bands. My older brothers say they like them the best. I can't figure out why. They only take up time, and they don't play any music. Mom said the girls could all catch their deaths of pneumonia the way they dress. I don't know why she said that. The sun was burning hot. I do think it might be fun to be the drummer in the back of the pickup beating out the rhythm they march to.

The drill team was trailed by what my dad called the "everyone who wanted to be in the parade, but couldn't find a float to ride" entries. These are kids on bikes, boys on skateboards, kids pulling wagons, children walking dogs, people dressed as clowns, or anything else that can take space on the street. Actually, they might sound stupid, but I don't mind them too much. There seems to be some kind of unwritten rule that if a person isn't an official "ride on the float" kind of person, then they have to throw candy to make their presence worthwhile.

Some children make pigs of themselves, even bringing bags to put their candy in. My dad always makes me stay on the sidewalk until the candy is thrown, so I end up with nothing but Halloween candy trick-or-treaters didn't want.

The most useless part of the parade has to be the politicians in big cars that have signs on them, which Daniel translated for me. The signs all said, "Vote for Dufus," no matter who was in the car. Politicians always throw the best candy. The problem is, they are so busy waving at the grownups that they never throw very far, and we smaller kids don't get any. Daniel said a politician is someone with a big mouth and weak mind, but I think he means weak arm.

The floats were next. A float, in the Ashton parade, is any trailer with anything on it and something written on the side. There was one that was simply an outhouse with writing on it. My dad said the writing was a politician's name, and some phrase about what kind of job he was doing.

Every major business in the town sponsored a float, so the parade was guaranteed to have at least five. These were always pulled by the best-looking pickups in town. John said he heard that some guys buy a nice pickup just so they can pull a float.

About halfway through the floats, everything came to a halt. One of the pickup drivers had forgotten to drop his wife's cookies at the baked food sale. He just parked in the middle of the street, got out, and took his food to the table. He said he was sorry it was late; he had forgotten, but he thought he better get it there before it got too cold, or his wife would be mad. He then went and got back in his pickup.

Someone yelled, "I hope you weren't the one that baked that, Joe!" and another person called "Hey, Joe, what's the problem? Won't your Chevy go? Maybe you should get a Ford!" Everyone laughed as he got back in his pickup so the parade could continue on down the street.

Blair laughed and rolled his eyes. "This would never happen in the Rose Parade. In fact, I doubt there would even be a baked food sale allowed along the street."

My dad informed him that the baked food sale is how we pay for the parade, and we all donate. I know that we help with the one at the 24th celebration. My dad always says he takes what my mom cooks to the baked food sale, and then pays a fortune to buy it back. I asked Blair how they paid for the Rose Parade, but he just laughed a "you are so stupid" kind of laugh.

The parade also included the machinery entries. First were the old cars and trucks. We tried to get them to blow their horns, which have a neat "barooga" kind of sound. Following the cars and trucks came the antique tractors. One of the old tractors died and wouldn't start back up, so a group of men pushed it off onto a side street so the parade could keep going.

The new farm machinery was after that. They always drive the newest, best-looking tractors and combines in all of the local parades. I always marvel at these. They are so big and beautiful. Blair turned to me and asked, "What are they driving that stuff in the parade for?"

"It's the newest farm equipment," I answered, trying to hold back my pride. "Isn't it neat?" I was sure this must beat out that stupid old Rose Parade he was bragging about.

"It is about the dumbest thing I've ever seen," Blair said.

I was just about to show him how dumb it was when my dad stepped between us and told my cousin that it was important to a farming community.

Blair made a face at me. "In the Rose Parade we have famous movie stars and everything."

I had just about had all I could take of his bragging. "You want to see stars?" I'll show you stars!"

I'm not exactly sure what that phrase means, but Daniel had said something like that once to a guy he was mad at.

My dad, however, didn't like it, and told me to "Simmer down!"

Blair leaned his head over where my dad couldn't see, and stuck his tongue out at me. So I stuck mine out back at him.

Finally, came my favorite part of the whole parade - the horses. I love the horses. Men and women came along dressed as cowboys and cowgirls on beautiful Morgans, quarter horses, Arabians, and Appaloosas. I may be small and not be that smart on everything, but I know most of the breeds by sight.

Sometimes someone brings a little colt tied to the saddle of its mother. I especially like them. One of the riders had the colt of the horse he was riding tied on along side. He stopped and let us come out and pet the little horse.

Blair couldn't believe this. He said it would never happen at the Rose Parade. I don't know anything about the Rose Parade, but it was beginning to sound mighty boring.

The whole parade didn't last all that long and Blair asked, "Is that it?"

"No," John answered, "Just keep watching."

Pretty soon, all of the parade came back from the other direction. They had all gone down and turned around in the church parking lot and started back. It was even more fun the second time, because we got to watch the drill team trying to dodge all of the horse droppings.

"Great! We get to watch the parade twice, just so it will be long enough to be called a parade," Blair grumbled.

After the parade was over, we went to the drug store, which was selling root beer floats for a dime. Dad loves root beer floats, so he bought one for each of us. There was also a group selling snow cones for a dime, but Dad said he couldn't see the use in paying money "for a bunch of ice."

As we drank our root beer floats, we headed to the park for the community events. These events included a good old-fashioned taffy pull, a greased pig chase, a greased pole climb, hamburgers and hotdogs, and lots of other good things to eat.

Of course, it had to start with a long talk. It seems that, for anything good, there has to be a price. In fact, that was the topic of the talk. I think he said he was talking about freedom, but I definitely could see other applications.

The first fun event was the taffy pull. I think they wanted to do that before everyone got too dirty. John and Jason are both strong, and they stretched their taffy out about the length of a long truck. In fact, Daniel had to get in the middle to make sure it didn't hit the ground. Then, after they stretched it, they looped it back and pulled again. Someone said it was to soften it. I just thought it was for fun. Watching the pulling is just about as much fun as eating the taffy. Well, actually, not near as much fun, but it is still fun.

My mom wouldn't let us eat any taffy until we had had some "real food," so my dad bought us each a hamburger. I liked these hamburgers because there were plenty of toppings, and we could put on all we wanted. I put on so many toppings I couldn't get my mouth over mine. When I squeezed it down to where my mouth would fit over it, the toppings went out the back. We had to settle for water to drink. With our big family, my dad said it was all we could do to afford the hamburgers. I wished I had saved my root beer float.

As soon as we were done eating our hamburgers, we were allowed to take a piece of the taffy. I got a big piece, ate some, and wrapped up the rest in a napkin to take home.

After lunch, it was time for the other events. The greased pole climb was first. On top of the pole was a ten-dollar bill. Whoever could climb to it got to keep it. I thought it was nice of all of the older kids to let us littler ones go first. I did notice that each successive person went a little farther than the last. And as soon as the kids started getting near the top, the older kids started clambering as to who would get to be next, and weren't so generous in allowing others ahead of them.

Jordan Harris, a skinny boy, whom everyone says is from a very poor family, was up. A person could tell that he really wanted the money. He jumped as hard and as high as he possibly could, and then he started climbing with every ounce of energy he had. He got within inches of the money, and then the grease was too much for him. He was trying so hard to reach the money that he lost his grip and fell. Everyone gasped, but some men jumped in and caught him.

My brother, Daniel, had his turn next. He isn't the biggest or strongest of our family, but he is one of the fastest. He made a clean jump, and moved quickly up the pole. Just as he hit the grease and was beginning to slip, he reached out with a lightening grab and had the ten-dollar bill. As he slid down the pole, everyone cheered him and slapped him on the back. He smiled, but I could see that he was looking somewhere beyond the crowd. I turned and followed his gaze, and I realized he was looking toward Jordan Harris. Jordan was standing to the side and seemed quite defeated.

As everyone was moving over to the greased pig chase, Daniel walked over to the hamburger stand. I thought he was going to spend some of the money. Instead, he just asked them if they could change a ten. He asked them for a five and five ones. Then, quietly, he walked over to Jordan and gave him a five and two ones.

"But," Jordan protested, "you are the one that earned it."

"We earned it," Daniel said. "You scraped off the grease so I could reach the top."

"But I can't take the biggest share," Jordan said.

"You've got to," Daniel said. "You're the one that has to clean the grease off his clothes."

They both laughed, and then Jordan, who was a couple of years younger than Daniel, smiled and they shook hands. As Daniel turned back to the greased pig chase, he saw me standing watching him. He simply shrugged. "He needs it more than I do."

As he walked past me, I thought about how we worked all day hauling hay, and when we went to weigh the loads, we couldn't afford the ten cent sodas in the machines. I'm sure a person could get a lot of orange sodas for ten dollars. They are my favorite. Thinking about what Daniel did, I felt funny as I followed him to join the crowd.

"To win, you've got to hang on to the pig until I count to ten," I heard the man in charge saying. "The winner gets to keep the pig and a five-dollar bill." I wondered how many orange sodas a person could get for five dollars.

He also said there were three categories: five to ten, eleven to fifteen, and sixteen and up. I was probably the smallest one in the first category. My mom didn't want me to do it. She said I would just get dirty and get myself hurt. However, I begged and begged, and my dad finally said I could. He told my mom that competition is good for a person.

We all got into the large, makeshift corral, and formed a semicircle around the gate where the pig was to be released. The men got the pig to the gate, and one held it, while a couple of others greased it up really well.

"Ready?" asked the announcer.

"Ready!" the men answered.

"Let her rip!" the announcer yelled.

As he yelled, a man swung the gate open wide. All of the older pig chasers ran forward, leaving the few of us five-year-olds, and Bobby Haws, far behind. We five-year-olds were too slow, and Bobby, well, he is about the biggest ten-year-old I have ever seen. I figure he probably weighs about as much as a yearling calf, or maybe even a small cow.

I couldn't even see the pig. As we ran up and down the circular pen, I still couldn't see the pig, only the direction all of the others were going. All of us five year olds were quite a ways behind everyone else, and Bobby was behind us.

Suddenly, the main group turned and headed our way. I saw one boy jump, and then another, and then another, and, in a big pink push, out of the crowd of people came the pig, heading straight for me.

He wasn't the biggest pig I have ever seen, but with him heading straight for me, he seemed like a monster. My brothers all started yelling, "Tommy, grab him! Grab the pig!" My mother was yelling, "Get out of the way! Get out of the way!" That sounded like the best advice, since, I think I mentioned, he was heading straight for me.

I started backpedaling as fast as I could go when that overgrown side of ham lowered its head and rammed me right in the chest. I threw up my arms to protect myself, and I felt the air go out of me as my body slammed to the ground. I felt something solid, like a stick, and I grabbed on to it.

There was a loud squealing as I felt myself jerked forward, as if I had caught hold of a rope tied to the bumper of a car. I had the pig by the leg. He was dragging me all over with the crowd of others right behind.

My brothers were all yelling, "Hold on! Hold on!" My mother was yelling, "Let go!" "Let go!" I could hear the announcer counting, "Three...four...five," and the pig squealing, "Weee! Weee! Weee!"

With every jump and kick, I could feel my hand slipping, as the pig dragged me a little slower, and a little slower. The others had nearly caught up to us now. We were headed straight for Bobby, and the pig was now going much, much slower with me holding onto his leg.

"Eight...nine..." said the announcer. We had almost come to a stop as the poor tired pig could move no further. At that very moment, Bobby jumped. The force of his jump jerked the pig's leg from my hands. As I looked up, the pig was now underneath Bobby, and all I could see were the four hooves spread out beneath him; the poor thing was all splayed out like he was ready to be cooked.

As I heard the announcer counting, "eight, nine, ten," I dropped back into the mud, totally crushed. I had tried so hard, and there was no way Bobby could have caught it if I hadn't slowed it down. Bobby just waited for it to go by and plopped on it, like an elephant on a kitten. I just laid there in the mud until my dad came and pulled me to my feet. I felt like crying, but I knew I was too old for that.

Bobby stood up too, but the pig didn't move. Either he was afraid someone else would jump on it, or its legs were all broken from laying under all that weight.

My dad took my hand and, as I walked toward the fence with him, the announcer called for another cheer for Bobby. I didn't feel much like cheering, but my dad always insisted on us being good sports, so I tried as hard as I could. The world seemed very blurry.

Then the announcer said, "Let's hear it for the little guy that hung on so hard! What a show of courage!"

Everyone cheered louder then than they did for Bobby, and my dad leaned down and said, "They're cheering for you, son. I don't think there is anyone here who doesn't feel you are the one who actually deserves that pig."

As my dad lifted me over the fence, Old Man Reynolds held out his hand. "Let me shake the hand of the little guy with the big heart," he said. As he shook my hand, I felt something solid. When he let go, I looked into my hand, and there was a silver dollar. I looked up at him, and he smiled and winked.

My dad said, "So, what are you going to do with that?"

I grinned through all the mud on my face. "I'm going to buy all of the orange sodas in the world!"

13

School

hen fall came, since I had turned six during the summer, Mom said it was time for me to go to school.

Fall is such a nice time of year. I always enjoy the cooler weather. In late August and September, the farmers are busy cutting grain. I love to go out by the augers that are putting the grain into the granaries, and smell the rich dust that fills the air. My older brothers tell me it is too dangerous for me to be there, but once the loud chang-chang-chang starts, I can pretend I can't hear them when they tell me to leave.

By then, the last hay crop is in, so I especially like to climb on the tall hay stack and look for miles in all directions. I always suck on a fresh piece of hay and let the juices run down my throat as I lay on my back and watch the clouds form and dance their stories across the big blue sky. I like to listen for the onk-onk of the geese that fly in their V formations heading south.

Life is so good in the fall. But the thought of school was both exciting and scary at the same time.

I decided it couldn't be too bad; I got a new pair of shoes. It was the first new pair of shoes I could remember. Before that, I always got hand-me-downs from my brothers. I don't mind them, but it is nice to have something new. I also got some new pants and two new shirts.

The only problem I have with new clothes is that I'm not supposed to get them dirty. I put them on and headed outside to show Tippy and Nosey. I had no more than stepped out the door than Mom told me to keep them clean. What's the fun in that? I ended up going back in and changing to old clothes so I could have fun.

Mom and Dad didn't send me to kindergarten. They said that kindergarten is just a year of play, and there was no way they were going to send their children to school to play. Life is for working. So the first day of school, Mom had to take me to the office to register. By the time I got to class, I was already late.

There were two first grade classes. I was assigned to Miss Markley's class. The principal led the way to the classroom, and while we walked, he told my mom that Miss Markley was "...just new out of school, with the best training in discipline, motivation, and teaching techniques."

As we came to the open door, I saw Miss Markley. She was pretty. When we stepped through the doorway into the room, everyone stared at me. I pulled back behind my mom. My mother took my arm and gently pulled me into the room, following the principal. The principal went up and talked to Miss Markley.

As I looked around the room, I realized how strange I must look. Everyone else was wearing new clothes too, but they were much different from mine. All of the boys, and some of the girls, were wearing pants that looked soft. They also had pretty, shiny looking shirts. Everyone also wore soft brown shoes, very different from mine.

My shoes were work boots two sizes too big. Mom bought them that way so I would have plenty of room to grow. My pants were tough Levis so that when they got old, I could use them for farm work; my shirts were flannel.

After the principal had visited with the teacher a minute, he left the classroom. Miss Markley said, "Boys and girls, we have a new student in our class. His name is Tommy Johnson." Then, pointing to a desk, she said, "Tommy, you can sit here by Marco." My mom led me over to the desk. She helped me get out my new erasers, pencils, and crayons. I noticed that I had the smallest pack of crayons of anyone in the class.

Everyone kept staring at me.

When my mom finished helping me, she excused herself. As soon as she left, Miss Markley said, "Tommy, we were just reciting the alphabet. Everyone else just finished; would you mind reciting it for us?"

Everyone kept staring at me. I wanted to run, but my feet wouldn't move.

Neither would my mouth. I couldn't do anything but shake my head.

"What do you mean, you won't say the alphabet?" Miss Markley asked. "You will do it if I say you will."

"I think he's too dumb," Marco said, mocking me. "He never came to kindergarten last year." With that, he hit me, almost knocking me from my chair. Everyone else laughed.

Miss Markley's voice was sharp. "That's enough, Marco." Then, turning to me, she said, "Tommy, the first thing you will learn is that you will answer me when I ask you a question. If you do not, you will sit in the corner. Do you understand?"

I nodded. "Do you understand?" she asked again. Again I nodded. "I can't hear you," she said louder. I tried to say yes, I truly did, but nothing came out.

Everyone was still staring at me.

"Probably too dumb to talk," Marco said, hitting me again, and everyone laughed.

Miss Markley's voice trembled with impatience. "That's enough, Marco. Perhaps you would like to sit in the corner yourself?"

Marco rolled his eyes. "Whatever."

Marco was bigger than most of the other children, and it was obvious that he had taken a special interest in me. I wish he hadn't.

It was also clear that Miss Markley was becoming exasperated as her voice was getting louder. She looked at me again. "Now, Tommy, I will give you one more chance. Say the alphabet."

I didn't have any idea what she was talking about, and I couldn't seem to open my mouth to say so. "Do you know the alphabet?" she asked. I shook my head. "I can't hear you," she said. I shook my head again.

Everyone was still staring at me.

"What a dummy," Marco said. "Dummy, dummy, dummy." He hit me again, and everyone laughed.

"Stop it Marco," Miss Markley yelled. Then, turning to me, she said, "I don't have time to be babysitting someone who should have learned the alphabet last year. Nor do I have patience to deal with someone who won't try."

Miss Markley walked back, grabbed me by the arm, and dragged me back to a small table in the back of the room. She gave me a picture and some crayons. "Here," she said. "Color this. I've got things to do." She stormed back to the front of the room and continued having the class say the alphabet.

I really didn't mind it in the back all that bad. Coloring was kind of fun, and Marco couldn't hit me. Also, no one was staring at me. Every once in a while, Miss Markley would say, "You want to work hard so you don't have to sit in the dumb section with Tommy." Then everyone would turn around and stare at me.

Other than that, I kind of liked Miss Markley. She let me do anything I wanted, as long as I was quiet. I sat there and colored or flipped through books and looked at the pictures. There was also a small sink in the back, and I could get a drink any time I wanted.

When the bell rang, everyone got up and headed out the door. "Is it time to go home?" I asked one of the girls closest to me.

"Of course not, Stupid," she answered. "It's time for recess."

When I got outside, I decided I would try to avoid Marco. It didn't take me long to find out why he was bigger than most everyone else in the class. He was a year older because he had been held back a grade. That is news that everyone talks about, especially him. He seemed proud of it.

I saw kids playing all sorts of games. Some were gathering up near a fence, choosing teams for a game called kickball. One of those doing the choosing asked, "Who's the new kid?" "Oh, don't choose him," one of the boys from my class said. "He's the class dummy." Soon, everyone was chosen except me. "Ok, let's play," someone shouted.

"What about Tommy?" I heard someone say. I turned and saw that it was Suzanne, Suzanne from church, Suzanne, the one with the beautiful black hair and brown eyes.

"Can't," the boy who was choosing teams said. "The teams are already even."

I saw Suzanne look around at the two teams, and then she said, "What do you mean they're even? They have eleven and we only have ten."

"Adding a dummy to the team is like taking one away, and then we would only have nine," the boy sneered.

"If he can't play, I'm not playing either," Suzanne replied.

"Suit yourself," the boy said. "It's not like you're all that good."

I could see Suzanne bite her lip, and then she grabbed my arm. "Come on. Let's go play tag." I found out that tag was fun, but I would look over at those playing kickball, running around the bases, throwing the ball, and everything, and I hoped that someday I could try it.

Later in the day, when the bell rang telling us it was time to go home, I wasn't sure what to do. Miss Markley asked me where I lived, and I explained the best I knew how, but it didn't help. "Does anyone know which bus Tommy is supposed to ride?" Miss Markley asked.

No one said anything.

"Can anyone tell me where he lives?" Miss Markley asked.

I knew some kids from church, but no one wanted to help because they didn't want anyone to know they knew me.

"I guess I'll just have to take you down to the office and find out," she said, sounding very annoyed. She started walking with me down the hall when we ran in to Suzanne.

Suzanne smiled at me. "Hi, Tommy."

"Hi," I replied.

"Do you know him?" Miss Markley asked, seeming somewhat surprised that someone did.

"Yes," Suzanne said.

"Can you help him get on the right bus?" Miss Markley asked.

"Sure," Suzanne answered. Miss Markley left, obviously happy to be rid of me.

There were two buses. Suzanne said we could ride either one. She said both of those buses dropped kids off around town, and then they met in front of the junior high, where a whole lot more buses joined them. There we had to switch to other buses that would take us home.

As we stood in front of the two busses, Suzanne asked, "Which bus would you like to ride?"

The buses each had a picture drawn on the side to help us tell them apart. One had a blue bird, and one had a bat. I saw Marco getting on the one with the blue bird.

"How about this one?" I suggested, pointing to the one with the bat.

"All right," Suzanne said, "bat bus it is."

I liked sitting by Suzanne. She is kind, pretty, and talks to me. When we got to the junior high, she showed me which bus I needed to ride. She said she knew because she saw which one my brothers and sisters rode. She rode a different one from there, and I was sad not to have her with me all the way.

I was glad to get home. When I arrived, Nosey and Tippy were there waiting for me. They had probably been chasing cars most of the day because they were right by the road.

After a couple of days of school, Miss Markley moved my desk to the back of the room to stay. She said I might as well just go right there because I wasn't smart enough to learn like normal kids.

When anyone else had to sit in the back, they always moved their chair as far away from me as possible. Even the kids from church did this. I couldn't understand why. At church they were friendly, but then in school, they pretended they didn't know me at all.

The first few weeks went by without too much trouble. I sat in the back and colored or looked at books. I did get a little bored. I wished Suzanne was in our class instead of in the other one so I would have someone to talk to. But I could day dream a lot. I would look out the window, and I often imagined I was running with Tippy and Nosey like I always had.

Playing tag at recess was a lot of fun, too. One day, a girl named Kathleen, from the other first grade class, came up to me. "You're kind of cute," she said. I could feel my face grow hot. I felt my insides do something that felt good, but funny. I started mostly chasing her during tag and she mostly chased me. I noticed that Suzanne looked a little left out. She would tag me, and I would chase her for a minute, and then I'd go back to chasing Kathleen.

After I was in school about a month, Marco got moved from our class to the other one. He talked back to Miss Markley a lot, and she didn't seem to know what to do about it. Mrs. Hillard, the other first grade teacher, was an older, more experienced teacher, so after a talk with the principal, Marco was moved.

I thought my life had just gotten better, but it went from okay to terrible. Now that Marco didn't have me to tease in the classroom, he made up for it at recess. To make matters worse, he was part of a group that were all his age or older. Some were in second grade and some were in third. They were called Rodney's gang. There were five of them. They would go all over, causing problems around the school. If someone built something, they would knock it down, and usually the builder, too.

Rodney was my next door neighbor, and even though he was almost three years older than me, we had played together now and then. I thought we were friends. I was wrong.

One recess, while we were playing tag, Kathleen was chasing after me when Rodney's gang came up, led by Rodney and Marco.

"What are you playing with that dummy for, Kathleen?" Marco said.

"What do you mean?" she asked.

"Oh, just that he's the dumbest kid in the whole first grade," Marco answered. "Maybe even the dumbest kid in the whole school."

"Really?" Kathleen said, looking at me.

"I hear he doesn't even know the alphabet," Rodney said.

"I didn't know that," Kathleen replied.

"Yeah," Marco added, "just ask Miss Markley. She makes him sit in the back away from **normal** people."

Led by Rodney, they all started chanting, "Dummy, dummy, dummy," with Kathleen joining in. Then Rodney came right up to me and shoved me down.

Suzanne jumped up between us. "Leave him alone!"

"Oh, what, you're sticking up for him?" Rodney taunted.

People gathered around, and I could feel that my face was hot. But this time, the feeling inside didn't feel good at all, and Rodney was threatening Suzanne. The bell rang, and everyone, except Suzanne, turned and headed to line up, leaving me sitting on the grass. Suzanne offered her hand to help me to my feet.

Once I got back to the classroom, and I was sitting in the back as usual, all I could think about was Kathleen's face when Marco said I was the dumbest first grader, and how she had joined them in calling me names.

When it was recess, I walked over to the freeze tag group. Kathleen met me just as I got there. "We don't want you to play with us anymore," she said. Then she turned back to their game, leaving me standing alone.

14

The Problem With Girls

 was no longer allowed to play tag. Kathleen ran the group. With her blond hair and her big blue eyes, most boys thought she was the prettiest girl in the school. As for me, I could never forget the look she gave me when Marco told her I was dumb.

I noticed that Suzanne quit playing tag, too. She played with some other girls with a little play house, pretending they were moms taking care of kids. I obviously couldn't play with them. We just quit playing together because everyone teased us about being boyfriend and girlfriend.

We even quit sitting together on the bus. She sat with her friends, and I sat alone. I don't think we actually planned it that way; it just happened. It wasn't that Suzanne wasn't nice to me, because she always was, and she would talk to me when others wouldn't. It's just that, after a while, it simply seemed easier than taking the teasing.

I'm not quite sure why boys aren't suppose to like girls in first grade, but another first grader, Steven, told me we weren't. He went to kindergarten, so he should know.

Some girls, like Kathleen, make it easy not to like them. She doesn't like me. She even makes it obvious that she's avoiding me. She crosses to the other side of the hall when I come and, if I say something to her, she ignores me.

I heard that most of the boys in the school have liked her at one time or another, but she eventually treated them kind of like she treated me.

There is one boy I know who isn't afraid to show he likes girls. In fact, it doesn't bother Mitch at all. He not only plays freeze tag, he plays kiss tag. That is disgusting. But he and about four girls play it almost every recess. They all chase him, or he chases all of them.

That is, he plays it every recess that he isn't out behind the storage shed with Wendy. I have never actually seen them do it, but everyone says they go out there and kiss. That's kind of gross. Actually, that's **really** gross.

I think that if you kiss a girl, you are supposed to marry her or something. But Mitch kisses lots of girls, and he doesn't seem to think he is married to any of them. Besides, I think you're only supposed to be married to one at a time.

During the summer, I got an invitation to Mitch's birthday party -- not from Mitch, but from his mom. That's because we go to the same church. At the birthday party, we all played some games for a while, and then it was time to eat the cake and open presents. But we couldn't find Mitch. His mom was frightened. She asked us to all help find him. Pretty soon, one of the boys came running in and reported that Mitch and Wendy were kissing behind the barn.

Wendy got sent home, and Mitch had to spend the rest of the afternoon in his room. I think it's because Mitch's mom thinks they are too young to be married.

We ate the cake and went home with a few goodies, but since Mitch was in his room, we never got to see the presents everyone had brought him. I don't even know what my mom sent with me, and I never did find out.

Anyway, I couldn't play with the girls at school, even though I think Suzanne is one of the nicest people in the world. I would swing or play on the slide or jungle gym, but as soon as I got on one of those, Rodney's gang would show up and knock me off. I spent a lot of my recess time trying to stay away from Rodney's gang.

Marco quit picking on me himself. He even seemed to feel bad for what he started, but I don't think he dared say so to the rest of the gang. Rodney, though, was another matter. He seemed determined to make my life miserable. I could expect to get pushed down at least once a day – more, if I wasn't careful.

Suzanne would stand up for me, but Rodney would always says, "Oh, you've got to have a girl protect you." As nice as Suzanne is, that is more embarrassing than getting knocked down, so I tried to not be near her when Rodney's gang would find me.

Rodney had never hit Suzanne or pushed her down. That was considered a wimpy thing to do. Guys just don't hit girls. But he threatened her at times. Then, one day, he came up to where the girls in Suzanne's group had set up some little branches as if they were picnic tables, and they were pretending to have a picnic.

Suzanne had drawn a picture with a beautiful scene that she was quite proud of. She is a very good artist. Rodney kicked his way through their little picnic area, saying, "Excuse us. Coming through. Coming through." I saw

Suzanne's picture get picked up by the wind and carried across the playground. I took off after it and caught it, but not before it was covered with mud.

I brought it back to Suzanne. She looked at it, and I could see she was going to cry. She turned to Rodney and said, "Why don't you leave us alone, you big jerk!" I felt horrible for her. She is the kindest, calmest person I know, and for her to ever call someone a jerk must have meant she was really upset.

Rodney had never been called a jerk before, and Suzanne was one of the few people who had ever stood up to him. Suddenly, Rodney reached out and pushed her really hard. She fell, hitting the playhouse and scraping her arm. I could see some blood on her arm, and I was angry.

I jumped between her and Rodney. "Leave her alone!" I hollered.

"Oh!" he said. "And who's going to make me? A wimpy first grader?"

"Well, at least I'm not a sissy that goes around picking on girls!" I yelled.

Instantly, Rodney's fist caught me in the mouth, and I went down flat on my back. "Sissy, huh?" he said. "We'll see who's the sissy."

I felt like jumping up and fighting, but two things stopped me. One was that my dad had always told me not to fight, and the second was because there were five of them. However, the others seemed embarrassed. I don't think they were embarrassed that Rodney hit me, but they were embarrassed because he had picked on a girl. I wouldn't have gotten much chance to fight anyway, because Miss Markley walked up.

"What's going on here?" she asked.

Rodney quickly replied, "Tommy is calling names."

"Calling names?" Miss Markley asked. "Like what?"

"He called me a sissy," Rodney said.

Miss Markley grabbed me by the arm and hauled me to my feet. "We don't allow name calling," she said, shaking her finger in my face.

Suzanne tried to say something to Miss Markley, but Miss Markley just said, "You stay out of this! I know a troublemaker when I see one, and I know how to deal with him without your interference!"

Even though it was my nose that was bleeding, she was sure it was all my fault. As Miss Markley dragged me into the building, I saw the substitute teacher of the other first grade class talking to Suzanne.

Miss Markley pulled me into the classroom. By the time she had gotten the paddle out, the bell had rung, and everyone had come in and sat down. I think she deliberately took a long time so she could make sure everyone got to see the punishment.

"Do you know why Tommy is getting the paddle?" Miss Markley asked the class. No one said anything, so she continued. "Because he was calling names and fighting."

"I wasn't fighting," I said.

"You what?" she said, turning to me.

"I wasn't fighting."

She looked at me with mud on my clothes and blood dripping from my nose, and said, "I can look at you and see you were fighting. What do you think I am, stupid or something?"

I thought it was beginning to look like a possibility. I didn't answer, but she seemed to know what I was thinking, and it made her even angrier. "Does anyone think Tommy shouldn't get punished?" she asked.

No one said anything. I know most of the class had seen what had happened, but no one wanted to cross Rodney's gang, and no one thought I was worth standing up for. I was glad Suzanne wasn't there because she probably would have said something and gotten herself in trouble too.

Miss Markley shoved me across an empty desk. Whack! Whack! "Two for calling names," she said. Whack! Whack! "Two for fighting," she said. Whack! Whack! Whack! "And three more for lying," she said, grabbing me by my arm and shoving me toward my desk. "Now, go sit down!" she yelled.

As I walked to my seat, everyone I passed turned and looked away from me. I felt tears forming in my eyes. I was trying hard not to cry. The paddling hurt a lot. Miss Markley could really hit. Marco had taken the paddle a few times and acted like it was no big deal, but he bragged that he had lined the inside of his pants with thick cardboard so he could hardly feel it.

But what hurt most wasn't the paddling, but that I got punished for trying to do the right thing. I thought to myself, "See if I ever help someone again."

"Why do I have to go to school?" I wondered. What had I learned in the past few months that I'd been here? I'd learned that if a person doesn't know how to read, he is stupid, and if he is stupid, nobody wants to be around him. I'd learned that if a person is tougher than someone else, he can run things. I'd learned that some people, like Kathleen, are nice when it suits them, and mean when it doesn't.

And then I started thinking how some people, like Suzanne, are always good and kind. She was nice to me even when others made fun of her. She was one of the prettiest, best liked girls in the whole school, but she was still my friend. She could be friends with any boy in the whole school, but she chose to be friends with me.

Suddenly, I felt good, even with my backside still stinging. I decided that I would always stand up for Suzanne, even if I got paddled again.

And that was the first time since school started that I even halfway felt good about who I was.

15

The Auction

e had to be up earlier than usual Saturday morning because there was an auction, and we had to have our chores done before we went. It was going to be a big event. Mrs. Levins had been in an accident, and needed some help paying her hospital bills. Everyone in the community was donating something.

Everyone loves Old Mrs. Levins. She is a sweet lady. Her husband passed away only a few years ago. She had not learned to drive through most of her life. Old Mr. Levins must have known that he was dying, because he insisted that she learn, and he spent much of his last few months teaching her.

She drives slower than anyone I know. The boys always bring their bikes to church and see if they can beat her to the top of the hill that is between her house and the church. I think it is about three quarters of a mile in distance because everyone calls it the "three-quarter mile hill" when they talk about it. Usually, Mrs. Levins is one of the last ones to leave church on Sunday, and as she gets into her car, the boys pull up beside her on their bikes.

The number of bike riders has grown to the point that they now fill the whole street. A boy is always considered a child until he can beat her to the hill. Some teenagers can get to the hill and back to the church before she gets to the hill. A few can even beat her to the hill on foot if they have a few seconds head start. My mom won't let me bring my bike to church to see if I can do it. She says it is silly.

In the winter, Mrs. Levins' car is a favorite for a sport everyone calls "hooky bobbin." Kids grab onto the bumper of a car and let it pull them down the road, sliding along the ice on their shoes. It can be dangerous, especially if the sun has melted a patch of snow on the road, making dry pavement. A person might be skiing along, and then it wouldn't be slick, so they would land on their face and get hurt. My dad told me if he caught me doing it, I'd be in big trouble.

One Sunday, instead of being last to her car, as usual, Mrs. Levins was one of the first out of the church. She had family coming, and she had to hurry to get home. Hurry, of course, meant she hurried to her car. Then she drove slowly all the way home. No one could pass her because of the hill between the church and her house, since there was no way to tell if a car was coming from the other direction. By the time she finally topped the hill, there was a line of cars nearly all of the way back to the church. But no one complained, because everyone loves Old Mrs. Levins.

Sometimes my mom sends me over to her house to do small chores. I love to go, especially in the winter when I go with one of my brothers to knock icicles off of her house. They never let me very near the house, worrying that an icicle might fall on me. Instead, I make snowballs and throw them at the higher ones. I am always excited when I hit one. When we are all done, we never get away without having a cookie. Mrs. Levins says she really likes to bake and to give cookies to small boys.

But one morning, she fell and broke her hip. She doesn't have a lot of money, so the community was holding an auction to help pay the bills.

Everyone seemed to have something to auction except me. I really love Old Mrs. Levins, but I couldn't think of anything to give.

"You could auction off Nosey," Daniel suggested.

That is ridiculous. That would be like auctioning off one of my brothers or sisters. I must admit that selling Albert had crossed my mind after he got me in trouble for the cats. But I doubted anyone would bid.

Some of the older boys in our community were auctioning off work, things like a yard mowing or something like that. But that didn't help me. Who would buy the work of a small boy?

After chores were done, I went out to sit with Tippy, and, as usual, Nosey showed up. While I waited for everyone else to get ready, Tippy and I sat in the shade by the house, and Nosey munched a few of Mom's flowers. I wanted to help so much that I finally went to see my Dad. He told me that if I truly cared about someone, I must be willing to give up something that is important to me.

I have some things that are important to me, things like my rock collection. I have some of the neatest rocks. I have blue ones, green ones, white ones with speckles, and some that are pure, shiny black. I love to take Dad's hammer out to our old rock pile and open up rocks to find out what they look like inside. Dad doesn't like it when I use his hammer that way. Most everyone tells me my rock collection is nice, but they say no one would pay for it. I didn't even ask Mom. Every time she helps me clean my room, she throws my rock collection out.

I also have a neat marble collection, steelies and crystals, some of which aren't even chipped. But no one seemed to think that would sell, either.

I tried to collect coins once, but I found that whenever someone had candy, I ended up spending my coin collection. So I gave up.

I went back out and sat with Tippy and Nosey. Then I saw something that made my heart jump in a strange sort of way. My old orange bike was leaning against the garage. It wasn't much, but it was a two wheeler, and I was learning to ride it. I loved that old bike. It was a hand-me-down, but it worked, and that was more than could be said for some hand-me-downs. My heart ached at the thought of giving up my old bike, but I so badly wanted to help Old Mrs. Levins.

I slowly rolled it over and parked it with the other things that were to be loaded for the auction. My brothers had super neat things they made in their shop classes. Against those, my old bike, with its peeling paint, looked sad. But it was all I had to offer.

I went in and gathered up all the money I could find in my drawer. I had two dimes and two pennies. I checked behind all of the cushions on the couch and found another nickel and a dime. Daniel helped me count it, and told me I had a total of 37 cents. I hoped that would be enough. I had seen many times when my Mom had made a cake for a church auction, and my Dad had bid to buy it back. I hoped I might be able to do the same thing with my bike.

When I got back outside, everything was loaded except my old bike. Dad was standing there waiting for me. "Are you sure you want to put your bike up for auction?" he asked. "You know we can't afford to buy you another one."

I told him I wanted to. He looked at me and then at the old bike, and then he gently lifted it into the back of the pickup. I climbed in the old car with everyone else.

"Why are you auctioning off your bike?" Albert asked.

"Because I want to help out," I told him.

"Well, don't plan on riding mine," he said.

When we got to the auction, the smell of bacon and sausage filled the air. The men had set up some old cook grills, the same ones they used for the Fourth of July breakfast. That was the first time I remembered that I hadn't eaten yet. Breakfast wasn't free, like on the Fourth of July, but we could get all we wanted to eat for two dollars a person or fifteen dollars for a family. Dad just paid the family price, which meant I could go back for as much as I wanted.

After breakfast, it was time for the auction to start. They began with the baked goods. Mom had made my favorite homemade candy. I was glad I had just eaten a big breakfast so I wouldn't be tempted to buy anything before my bike came up. Soon they were winding up the jams and jellies, and it was time for the other things.

They started auctioning off the boys' labor. Frank Angstrom was doing a whole lawn mowing. I could see that the bidding on this was not equal since yards are not all the same size. The winning bid went to Old Man Angstrom. He had to outbid Mr. Jensen to save his grandson. It would take Frank a month to mow Mr. Jensen's lawn. He had the biggest yard in the county. In fact, my dad says his yard is half the county.

After that, I heard some of the other boys say they wished they hadn't put in work for bid. One of them got to clean a whole barn for a bid of two dollars, and it was the Wright's barn. It has a hundred individual cow stalls.

It wasn't long before the work was all auctioned off. Even some of the girls auctioned off work for a house cleaning or babysitting. Dad and Mom didn't let any of my brothers or sisters auction off work. They said they needed them at home too much.

After the work, it was time for the hard goods. First came some record players. I had heard a record player once at my friend's house. We had one, but it didn't work. I hoped my Dad would bid on one, but he didn't. With our big family he always says there is not a lot of money to spare.

Next, the auctioneer brought out my old bike. "How much for this old bike?" he asked.

My dad had told me to never be the first to bid. I am not sure why, but he always let someone else start. However, I couldn't help myself. I yelled out, "twenty-five cents." I saw my Dad look over at me, and wondered if he disapproved.

"Thirty cents," someone shouted.

"Thirty-five," I said.

"This is your bike, isn't it son?" the auctioneer asked.

"Yes, sir," I answered.

"Is it a good one?" he asked.

"It works."

"Forty," someone shouted.

"We've got a bid of forty, son," the auctioneer said. "Would you like to bid some more?"

"I only got thirty-seven cents," I answered.

I turned and walked away. As soon as I got through the crowd and around the pickup trucks where no one would see me, I took off running to our old car. I ran around to the side away from the auction and threw myself on the ground, breathing hard to keep from crying. I knew I was too old to cry.

I heard the auctioneer shout, "Sold! To..." and his voice faded out.

I didn't want to go back to the auction. Usually the thirty-seven cents would have made me excited to see what I could buy, but there was nothing else I wanted nearly as much as my bike. Later on, though, I thought I might like to say goodbye to it. But I couldn't see it as I wandered around the auction area. Whoever bought it had already packed it up.

By that time, they were getting to the quilts that the women had made. The quilts went for a lot of money. Most sold for about twenty dollars, but one even went for twenty-nine. That one was a very special quilt. Every woman in the community had embroidered their family brand on a square, and then the women had quilted all of the squares together. Everyone had to check it out. It was beautiful, and every family would have loved to have it, but eventually Mr. Olsen bought it.

The auction continued on for quite a while. The last things to be auctioned were the animals. People had brought pigs, sheep, chickens, and even a gentle old horse. When the Dalton boys brought in the big, old boar, it was quite a sight. There were four boys on two ropes. The two ropes were tied to the pig, and the boys, two per rope, were out front on each side, dragging the pig into the auction. The pig was not very cooperative and kept trying to break away. He was big, though, and fetched a good price.

The auction ended, and it was time to go home. Albert was first to join me at the car.

"Where have you been?" he asked.

"Nowhere," I answered.

"Too bad you couldn't afford to buy your bike," he said.

"Who bought it?" I asked, trying to act like it didn't matter.

"Len Wright," he replied.

Len Wright was one of Dad's good friends. I wondered why he would want it. It was way too small for any of his older boys, and his younger children were all girls, none of whom would be caught dead on such an ugly old bike.

Albert must have known what I was thinking, because he said, "He probably bought it for a nephew or something. He paid two dollars and fifty cents for it."

Suddenly, I felt good. I didn't know it was possible to feel bad and good at the same time, but the bike went for far more than I thought it might. I figured that much money would probably pay almost half of Old Mrs. Levins's bill.

When I got home, Tippy and Nosey were waiting for me. I had been going out in the pasture with them lately and practicing riding my bike. I like to go there because it didn't hurt as much as falling on the gravel road. Besides, Mom doesn't let me ride on the road.

Tippy and Nosey expected us to head out to the pasture as usual, but I didn't feel like it. I looked over at the empty spot where I would park my bike, and I just ran as fast as I could out to the haystack. That is where I go when I want to be alone. I like to go out there because it is high up. Tippy followed me up, and Nosey worked his way up, too.

As Tippy came up to me, he seemed to sense something was wrong, and he just laid his head in my lap. Nosey came and pushed against me, wanting to play.

I put my arm around him, and told him it wasn't a good day, but he didn't seem to understand. I sat and watched the clouds slowly drift overhead. Usually this made me feel better, but this time they all looked like bicycles.

I heard someone calling my name, so I hurried to the house. Albert told me that Len Wright wanted to talk to me.

"To me?" I questioned.

"Yes," he said, "and you better hurry, because he's been here awhile."

I ran out front, and there stood Mr. Wright, and with him was my old bike.

"You know," he said to me, "I got this old bike home, and I'll be darned if it isn't too small for me to ride."

I looked up at him, surprised that he didn't realize that before he bid on it.

"I was just wondering," he continued, "if you would like to buy it back."

I told him I would, but that I didn't have that much money.

"Well," he said, "I might be willing to trade for something valuable."

By now, my heart was thumping hard. I hurried into my bedroom and grabbed my treasure box. I took it outside to see if we could work out a deal. I opened it up and showed him what I had and he said, "Tell me about them."

I pulled out my crystal marbles and told him how I had gotten them from Buster in exchange for a piece of candy. I showed him how they gave a rainbow of color when you held them up to the light. Even the cracked ones sparkled in the bright afternoon sun.

I pulled out my rocks and showed him the deep blue inside on some that I had cracked open. I also showed him the one that had golden sparkles on white. I had half of a pretty blue robin egg. I had some pigeon feathers from the barn. I had a small clump of Nosey's wool that I had gotten off of the garden fence where Nosey had sneaked in to munch on Mom's carrots. I had some hair from Tippy from when I brushed him, and I had an almost perfect starling nest I had found in an old granary. As I took out each item, I explained to him why it was so neat. When I finished, I held the box out for him.

He looked at me and said, "I couldn't take all of these for the bike. That wouldn't be fair. How about fifteen cents, the two cracked crystals, one steelie, this pretty blue rock, and four pigeon feathers."

I couldn't even talk, so I just nodded. I ran in to get him a bag to put them in. We placed the things carefully into it, and he took it and handed me the bike. I excitedly took it and turned to go away, when he said, "Oh, just one more thing."

I turned to look at him, and he reached out his hand. "Friends forever?"

I took his hand, shook it. "Friends forever," I said.

Then I jumped on my bike and headed out through the pasture with Tippy and Nosey right behind me.

16

Brian Bearclaw

When I came back to school on Monday, I hadn't been in my seat very long when the substitute teacher of the other first grade class came into our room. She was the one who had helped Suzanne when Miss Markley was dragging me into the school. Her name was Mrs. Sange. She went to the front of the room and talked to Miss Markley. They looked back at me, and I could tell they were talking about me.

They came walking back to where I was. By then, the whole class was there, and everyone was staring.

"Mrs. Sange was wondering if you would like to transfer into her class," Miss Markley said. I thought about how Marco was over there, but I remembered that Suzanne was, too. "She thinks she might be able to help you learn to read," Miss Markley continued. I could tell by the way she said it that she thought it was an impossibility.

I thought to myself, "Everyone knows I can't learn to read," but I didn't say anything.

They helped me gather my things, and I moved to Mrs. Sange's room before school started. Mrs. Sange was only substituting for Mrs. Hillard, but it looked like she might be teaching for a few months. Everyone said Mrs. Hillard was having an operation of some kind.

Mrs. Sange let me sit in a seat next to Suzanne. Suzanne leaned over and whispered, "I told Mrs. Sange what happened Friday. Did you tell Miss Markley?"

"She wouldn't let me," I answered.

I almost told her I got the paddle, then decided against it.

I didn't like being in a new class again because everyone stared a lot. But at least I already knew many of them.

For reading, we were divided into four groups. I was in group four. Mrs. Sange called up our reading group first and told us to turn to page 32. I understood numbers, but I couldn't read them, so it didn't help at all. Mrs. Sange asked the person next to me to help me get to the right page.

"Ok," Mrs. Sange said, "Tommy, let's hear you read a little."

I didn't move or say anything. "Go on," she encouraged, "just sound it out." I still didn't move.

Suddenly, Marco said, "Oh, give it up. He's the dumbest kid in first grade. He doesn't even know his alphabet."

"Marco," Mrs. Sange said, "we'll have none of that in this class room."

"Well, it's true," Marco said.

"It's never true that someone is dumb," Mrs. Sange said. "It's just that some people are more blessed than others." Then she turned to me and asked, "Do you know the alphabet?" I shook my head. "Why don't you go ahead and go back to your seat, and maybe I can help you at recess."

I went back to my seat, and Marco mouthed, "Stupid" to me as I passed him. At recess, everyone else went out, but Mrs. Sange made me stay in for most of it. That was only half bad because I didn't have to have a run-in with Rodney and his gang, but I really missed being outside. She showed me letters and had me pronounce them and their sounds.

I thought the whole thing was crazy. I knew I couldn't learn to read; I knew I was too stupid. Everyone knew that.

It was only a couple of weeks before Christmas by the time I was moved to her class, but it seemed like forever until Christmas break.

I even began to hate Mrs. Sange, and I hated school even more. Why couldn't she just leave me alone? Why couldn't she just let me color like Miss Markley did? Even though I didn't like Miss Markley after what had happened, I began to think she must like me more than Mrs. Sange. Mrs. Sange couldn't seem to understand that I was too stupid to learn to read.

Besides, when I was sitting in the back coloring, no one bothered me. When Mrs. Sange was trying to get me to read, I was always embarrassed. People stared at me, and Marco was always saying something or jabbing me. Sometimes I hated school so much I felt sick.

Mrs. Sange just wouldn't give up. She kept having me come up with group four and having me try to sound out the words, but I knew I couldn't do it.

The only good reason for going to school was to see Suzanne, but we couldn't even talk, or everyone teased us. We weren't actually boyfriend and girlfriend like some of the boys and girls -- just friends. She always mouthed "you can do it," when I headed up with my group, but I knew I couldn't.

I was so happy for the day of the Christmas party. I knew the next day would be Christmas break, and I wouldn't have school for almost two weeks. The party was fun. We each brought a small present, like a box of pencils or crayons. We randomly traded them, and no one had any idea which one they would get. I got my gift from Lori, and it was a small book of dot-to-dot.

"Little good that will do," Marco said. "He doesn't even know his numbers."

"Marco," Mrs. Sange warned in a threatening voice, "that will be quite enough of that."

The food was good, and we played some fun games. When we finished and were getting ready to go home, Suzanne slipped me a little box. When I opened it, there was a beautiful picture she had drawn, and the most beautiful matchbox car. There was something written on the picture. Oh, how I wished I could read it. I didn't dare ask anyone to read it to me, afraid it might say something they would tease me about.

I had been working on a card for Suzanne for a couple of weeks. I can't draw as well as she can, and I was embarrassed about it. But I had drawn some flowers on it, mostly tulips because they are easy. I wished I could write and tell her how glad I was that she was my friend, but I couldn't. I did odd jobs for my brothers for a week to earn some money. They paid me a penny for each one. I saved five cents, just enough for a pack of gum. I put that inside the card and taped it shut.

I tried to sneak it to Suzanne when no one was looking, but Marco saw. "Oh, how sweet," he smirked. "A couple of love birds." I could feel my face grow hot. I was surely glad it was Christmas vacation.

Tippy and Nosey and I spent a lot of time together over Christmas. Tippy and Nosey still chased cars no matter how much I tried to break them of it.

Sometimes they chased together and sometimes separately. When Tippy was chasing by himself, no one even took a second glance. But when Nosey was chasing cars, people slowed way down. Nosey is usually following Tippy, and it looks like a lamb is chasing a dog. Some of the neighbors mentioned that they laugh when they see the lamb come out from hiding behind the old car, baaing after them.

For Christmas, I saved Tippy some cream and a bone. I gave Nosey some extra grain and a really nice piece of hay. I spent most of Christmas day playing with my new toys, but I did take some time to go outside and build a snowman with them.

Christmas vacation seemed very short. I didn't even enjoy it that much because I was so worried about going back to school. It didn't seem long before I was again waiting for the bus with Tippy and Nosey by my side.

However, when I got to school, there was a surprise. There was a new boy who took the desk right behind mine. Mrs. Sange introduced him as Brian Bearclaw. He was an Indian boy from the Dakotas. We immediately became friends, partly because we both enjoyed the out-of-doors, and partly because he couldn't read, either.

Brian and I played together at recess, and Rodney and his gang came over to cause trouble.

"I see the two school dummies are playing together," Rodney taunted.

"And what of it?" I said, as Brian stood up beside me.

Rodney wasn't used to being talked back to at all, and he pushed me. Before he could blink, Brian had pushed him back so hard that he went down flat on his back. Rodney hadn't even pushed me down, but Brian sure did Rodney.

"So you want to fight, huh?" Rodney growled, jumping up and doubling up his fists, as the other four in his gang came up beside him. I stepped back up beside Brian, and neither of us flinched as we faced them.

It was the first time more than one person had stood against them, and Rodney faltered. I think he was beginning to think about it. Brian and I might be younger than they were, but we were the two biggest first graders, and probably stronger than any one of his gang. His gang would help him, but he was in the front, and he would take the first blows. I think, for the first time, he may have wondered who would come out on the worse end of things. Suddenly he whirled around and marched away. "Come on, guys. They ain't worth our time."

After that, Rodney and his gang only called us names from a distance. They never pushed us around. This seemed to be a big blow to how much everyone around school feared them.

I didn't actually want to fight against Rodney and his gang; after all, there were so many of them. But when he picked on Suzanne, I knew if he did anything to one of my friends again, I probably would. It was strange how much more courage I felt when I didn't stand alone, or when I had someone to stand up for.

Brian and I played together a lot. We mostly dreamed of running away. Brian told me stories of living on the Indian reservation, where he spent his days hunting and fishing. None of his family, and very few of his friends, could read or write. They had never been to school. That was why he came out here. He came to live with another family so he could go to school.

He didn't think learning school stuff was important and hated it all. We talked about my joining him and taking Tippy and Nosey and going back to the Dakotas. We would live in the mountains, and fish and hunt to survive. We wouldn't have to put up with other people, especially people like Rodney.

The only problem with this was that sometimes, as we planned, I thought about leaving Suzanne, the only person who was my friend before Brian came. Brian and Suzanne had not become friends. Brian didn't feel a girl was worthy of being a friend, saying that in his village, that was how it was. Suzanne tried to be friends with him, but he just ignored her. That was the only thing that bothered me about Brian.

When it was free reading time, Brian and I always chose the same book. We didn't know what it was about, but it had pictures of forests, animals, rivers, and mountains. The more we looked at it, the more we dreamed of running away. Someday we would, and then to heck with the rest of the world.

17

Bossy

Brian made school bearable, but I still looked forward to the weekends. Spring was coming, and it was getting warmer. It was a beautiful morning in early March, and I just had to go outside. There was still a lot of snow on the ground, but mud puddles were starting to show up here and there.

I thought I would take a walk through the pasture and see if I could find some wild flowers. Once in a while, there was a small one that braved the snow and poked its head up early. I knew my usual luck would mean that if I found anything, it would likely be a bunch of wild onions, but even they are fun to chew on.

I got my coat on and went out, calling for Tippy and Nosey. I didn't see them anywhere, so I decided to walk alone. I could hear a meadowlark singing. Daniel said he heard that their mating call is meant to tell the world it is almost springtime. He said they sing, "Hello there, only ten days 'til spring." I think whoever told Daniel that is a real idiot. Everyone knows that it is a lot longer than 10 days to spring when they first start their mating calls. But I still love to hear them sing.

Spring is my favorite time of year. It means the warm days of summer are ahead. Everything starts out new, and the cold air smells good. Besides that, there are always lots of mud puddles to splash in.

I reached the pasture, and there was still no sign of Tippy and Nosey, even though I called them over and over. I climbed over the fence and started on my way across the pasture. The pasture looked like an alien landscape. There was still a lot of snow everywhere.

Little ice mounds jutted up all around where the cows had chosen to relieve themselves. The cow pies kept the snow underneath from melting. When everything started to thaw, these little mounds lasted longer. I love to walk through the pasture and kick the manure piles off of them so they'll melt. I often imagine myself a famous kicker on some football team.

I was wandering all around the pasture kicking the ice mounds, getting farther and farther out, when I heard a sound that scared me to death. The sound was the snorting of a cow that was ticked off at something. I turned, and there stood Bossy, snorting and pawing the ground, and I knew I was what she was ticked off at.

Bossy is usually a very gentle cow, but she had gotten her name for a couple of reasons. She was pretty much the boss of the herd. Every time we feed the cows and Bossy comes along, all of the other cows move out of her way and let her have first eats. The other reason was because she doesn't like anyone around her calf.

Anyone that came close learned that in a hurry. I could see from the shape of things, that shape being that Bossy wasn't as round as she had been, that I was probably in big trouble. In addition, I could see a small, black head poking up behind Bossy, barely outlined against a white patch of snow.

I froze with fear. Somehow, I had wandered by them and never even noticed. Now they stood between me and the fence. I knew I couldn't outrun her. She was the fastest bag-swinging, cud chewing, milk bucket on four legs. When she had a calf to defend, she could place in the Kentucky Derby.

I just stood there, hoping this was all a mistake, and that she actually hadn't noticed me. But that wasn't the case because, with one big snort, she charged.

Although I wasn't able to head for the fence, there was nothing I could do but run, unless I wanted to get run over. I was running with all my might, but I could hear her pounding hooves getting closer and closer. Just when I thought I was finished, I heard an "a-woo! a-woo!" Tippy was coming full speed across the pasture, clumsily tripping over cow pie mounds on his way.

Just as I felt Bossy's breath on my back, Tippy jumped on her head, catching her by surprise. I don't know how she hadn't seen or heard him coming. He made as much noise as a herd of buffalo. She must have just had me in her horn sights.

As far as cows go, Bossy is smart, and no one has to tell her that a dog is more of a threat to her calf than a boy is. She turned to face Tippy, who was now down on his belly. I don't know if he decided it made him a smaller target, or if he thought he was playing a game.

As they faced off, I took the time to run way around them, putting me on the other side of Bossy -- the fence side -- and I headed for safety.

Tippy was doing a good job of distracting her. She would bellow and charge, and at the last minute, he would jump to the side like a famous bullfighter as she went slipping and sliding to a stop a short distance beyond him. It almost looked like Tippy was enjoying this game. I was almost to the fence, glancing back now and then to keep an eye on them, when something went terribly wrong.

Bossy charged and, just as Tippy jumped to get out of her way, he tripped on a cow pie mound. It was just enough so that Bossy caught him with one of her horns and sent him flying. She slid to a stop and turned to face him again. Tippy laid there, motionless. I knew that if she reached him, she would kill him. I also knew I couldn't get there in time and didn't know what I'd do if I could. I considered what I would have to do if I wanted to save my dog. It scared me to death, but the thought of her killing Tippy, especially after he had come to my rescue, gave me more courage than I even knew I had.

I grabbed a small stick that was on the ground, and instead of heading for Bossy, I headed for her calf. I was almost there when Bossy charged toward Tippy. I had learned from my brothers how to imitate many cow and calf sounds, so as Bossy charged, I let out a calf-in-trouble beller. It may not have been perfect, but it was enough. Bossy slid to a halt just a few feet from where Tippy lay.

She looked in my direction, and then back at Tippy. Cows have a natural hatred toward dogs, and she seemed determined to continue her attack on him. But I quickly reached her calf, and I let out the troubled beller again, whipping her calf onto his feet. His frightened bawling mingled with my sounds. It was a desperate move, but I was desperate and didn't know what else to do.

At the sight of her calf and the sound of the bellering, Bossy turned and charged toward me. I headed for the fence, and she headed to cut me off. I was banking on the fact she would run to her calf, but Bossy is never predictable. I soon realized that I was not going to make the fence before she reached me, and I knew Tippy wasn't going to be able to come to my rescue this time.

Suddenly, I saw a white ball of wool shoot out from under the fence and head straight for Bossy. Nosey angled so he rammed Bossy on the side of one of her front legs, causing it to hook behind her other one. Down she went, end over end.

She lay there for a minute, stunned. Nothing had ever upended her before. She glanced briefly at the three of us, as if she didn't know which one to go after. Her mind seemed to turn back to Tippy. She struggled to her feet and turned toward him.

Nosey was back at her in an instant. He dodged right underneath her. She kicked out at him, bellowing and flipping around trying to catch him with her head. But Nosey was good at this game. He had gone through it many times in the new lamb pen as he darted around with the old ewes after him.

I turned and ran for Tippy. He was laying there, dazed, but still alive. I pulled on him. "Come on, Tippy, come on," I said, trying to drag him to his feet. I knew I couldn't carry him. He had to walk. With some coaxing, he roused and gradually wobbled to a standing position.

By this time, Nosey had run for the fence with Bossy right behind him. He darted through a hole and Bossy slid to a stop. She turned back to us. "Run, Tippy, Run!" I yelled. Tippy couldn't run. He was still too dazed. He could only wobble at a slow lope.

Bossy pawed some snow, then charged. Her charge was slower now. The tumble that Nosey had given her had really humbled her. But she began picking up speed as she came. I was waving my stick and shouting, but she was heading straight for Tippy, and I couldn't get her attention. She wasn't too far from me when a white streak shot past me.

Again, Nosey, with deadly aim, caught her on the side of the leg. She wasn't running nearly as fast, and only stumbled this time. Once more, she turned to face the lamb. He darted in and out of her legs as she kicked and bellowed. He was like a giant white fly, and she seemed determined to swat him.

Eventually he turned and raced for the fence with Bossy right behind. This had given Tippy and me enough time to also reach the fence farther down. I slipped between the wires. Tippy would normally jump over the net fence and below the first wire, but due to the throw he had taken, he didn't have the strength.

Bossy had finished chasing Nosey through the fence again, and stood there, snorting for a second. Then she turned and headed our way. "Come on,

Tippy. Come on," I said, "You can do it." Tippy just didn't have the energy to get over the fence netting. We've come too far, I thought. I grabbed the bottom of the net wire and, with all the strength I had, I pulled. It was just enough for Tippy to squeeze under while wriggling on his belly.

Bossy came sliding to a stop at the fence and snorted at us. She turned and started away, heading back to her calf, as Nosey joined us. I yelled after her, "So there, you big bag of hamburger!" Instantly, she turned and headed for the fence in our direction. She was going full steam, and it didn't look like she was going to stop for the fence. We fell all over each other as we scrambled away. Bossy slid to a stop just at the edge of the fence. As we picked ourselves up again, she let out a couple of snorts like she was laughing, and as if to say, "So there, you stupid boy!"

As she trotted away once more, I finally felt like I could breathe again. I put an arm around each of my friends, and said, "Let's go home."

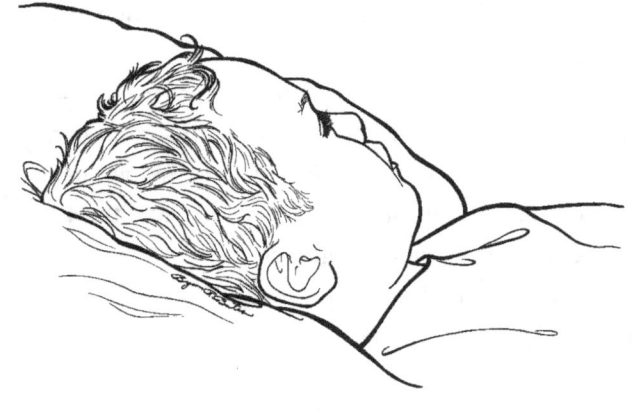

18

Friends Forever

ince Brian came, I had almost looked forward to going to school. But on Monday, Brian didn't come to school. With him gone, Rodney and his gang began to get meaner. Brian didn't come again on Tuesday, and Rodney and his gang started bothering me again. Rodney pushed me down, and Suzanne tried to stand up for me. Rodney just laughed and walked away.

He didn't hurt Suzanne anymore because it made him look stupid the last time, but he would knock over the toys and things she and the other girls played with. By Wednesday, I was very lonely. I spent most of the recesses trying to avoid Rodney and his gang. He still found me, and I still got pushed around.

I began to wonder where Brian was. Had he run away without me? Was he sick? I had to know. I finally went to Mrs. Sange and asked her. She told me that things didn't work out for him here, and he had gone back home to the Dakotas.

I felt sick. All day long, I could think of nothing else. Who would I talk to? Who would stand up with me against Rodney and his gang? When I got up Thursday morning, I had made up my mind that I was going to tell Mom I didn't ever plan to go back to school again. If Brian and his friends didn't have to go to school, neither did I. At breakfast, I was trying to think of the best way to say it, when the phone rang. My mom answered it, and after saying hello, she said, "He what?" She listened a minute and then said, "You're serious?!" My mom hurriedly handed the phone to my dad and ran out of the kitchen sobbing.

My dad took the phone and said hello. Then he said, "What happened?" After a brief pause, he said, "I see." I saw a look come over my Dad's face, one I had never seen before. He then said, "Thank you for letting us know," and hung up the phone.

"What is it, Dad?" John enquired.

My dad choked and tried to answer, but couldn't get the words out. He swallowed hard and tried again, but still couldn't. Finally, with his voice shaking, he said, "Len Wright had an accident and died last night." Then Dad turned and left the room.

Of all of our neighbors, Len had always been my father's best friend. I could remember many a time the two of them helped each other with something. Len often came over to help with the animals. When we branded, he helped us. When they branded, we helped them. Part of our property joined his, and there were times that we worked on those sections of fence together.

When our cows got into his pasture, Len never got mad. We got them back into our place, and he helped us fix the fence. He was always good and kind to everyone. His older daughters were my sisters' friends. Everyone who knew Len loved him.

One time, when Nosey was sick and Dad wasn't around, I didn't know what to do. I wanted to call a vet, but Mom said we didn't have money for that. I finally went to Len for help. He came over right away.

Nosey, being his typical self, had broken his way into the granary and had eaten too much. His stomach was huge, and he was lying on the ground on his side, panting for breath. Len knew right away what was wrong.

"He's bloated," he told me. "If we don't get the pressure in his stomach released immediately, he will die." He mixed up a lamb bottle full of mineral oil and turpentine, the same thing we gave the cows when they bloated.

Nosey was not about to take that stuff, so Len had to hold him with one hand and force the bottle into the back of his mouth with the other. It would drizzle into Nosey's throat, and he was forced to swallow. When he finished the bottle, Nosey acted like he was going to charge Len, but the pain was too much and he flopped down.

"We can't let him lie down," Len said. "We've got to keep him on his feet and get him to walk, if possible."

It was almost impossible to get him to walk, but Len helped me keep him on his feet while the medicine had time to work. As Len was holding him, he would stroke Nosey's head and talk to him. At first Nosey would swing his head around and butt at Len, but as the medicine started working, and Nosey began to realize Len was helping him, he would rub his head gently against Len. Len stayed with Nosey and me for a long time until Nosey was almost totally better.

One other time, Daniel changed the oil in the car and left it in a pan, and Nosey drank it. He was lying down groaning when I found him. I had no idea what was wrong with him. None of my older brothers could figure it out either. I didn't know what to do, so I went to Len.

Again, he came right over. He took one look at the black ring around Nosey's mouth, smelled his breath, and said, "Did he drink some oil?"

Daniel checked, and found the oil pan empty. Len helped us mix up some soapy stuff, which he made Nosey drink. He said it would help move it through his system. My brothers made a lot of jokes about Nosey "being well lubricated," "maybe we should change his filter while we were at it," and "maybe we should check the oil level on the little dipstick," but I was worried about my lamb and didn't think it was all that funny.

Len told us that all we could do was watch over him, try to make him comfortable, and hope it cleared itself out. A few hours later, Nosey was feeling better. He was up and moving around some, although he didn't eat anything for a few days. Mom got mad at Nosey because everywhere he went to the bathroom during the next few days everything died. There were dead flowers, dead plants in the garden, and dead spots in the lawn. It was most noticeable in the lawn, where we had little circles of dead grass here and there.

Len had probably helped everyone in the family at one time or another, so when Dad left the room that morning, it suddenly became very quiet. One by one, we all just got up from the table and silently went to work. No one was hungry any more.

As I went out to do my chores, I saw my old orange bike sitting in the shed. I remembered how Len had bought the bike at the auction and brought it over to me. I don't know what happened to me, but I kicked the bike as hard as I could. It hurt my foot, and my bike clattered to the ground, but it seemed to help me feel better, so I kicked it again and again and again. When I ran out of breath, I just fell on the ground and breathed hard to keep from crying, but the tears came anyway.

I tried not to let them, afraid Albert might come by and call me a sissy, but I couldn't help it. By this time, Tippy and Nosey had found me. They nuzzled me as if to ask what was wrong. As I stroked Nosey's soft, white neck, I thought about how I wouldn't still have my little friend if hadn't been for Len.

That was when I thought of something I wanted to do. I knew I had to get my chores done first, so I hurried and fed the calves and helped with the straw. Mom and Dad said we didn't have to go to school that day if we didn't feel like it. I didn't feel like it. I got out some paper and colored pencils and worked hard all day coloring. I tried and tried, but it never seemed just right. I would rip up the paper and start again. I worked on it until Mom got worried. I hadn't gone outside or done anything else all day.

The next day, Mom and Dad insisted we had to go to school. It was Friday, and they thought we should go to catch up any work we needed to do before the weekend. I said I shouldn't have to go to school if Brian didn't, but Mom and Dad made it clear I would.

I got permission to stay inside from recess and work on my paper. Mrs. Sange usually felt we should get at least a little fresh air, but she knew of Len's death, and she said I could do what I wanted. That also kept me away from Rodney and his gang, and I didn't feel like facing them.

Friday night, Mom and Dad went alone to the viewing. The funeral would be on Saturday. We seldom go to a funeral as a family, unless it is a relative, but Mom and Dad decided we all could go if we wanted. I knew I had to have my paper ready before I went.

I hurried and got my chores done after school, and then I set to work on my paper again. It was looking more like what I wanted it to be. I finally had the pictures drawn, but I wanted to write something on it. I didn't want anyone else to read it, so I would ask Daniel how to write a word. He would write it onto a paper for me, and then I would copy it onto my paper.

I had already been told to go to bed many times before I finally felt like the paper was finished. I lay in bed much of the night thinking about Len. I was glad it was dark and no one could see me cry.

Saturday, as soon as our chores were done, I got dressed in my nicest suit. I carefully folded the paper and put it in my suit coat pocket.

Usually, when we go to funerals, Mom and Dad visit with the family while we children go straight to the chapel. I asked if I could go with them to visit with the family, and they let me. It was a long line, and while we stood there, I pulled out the paper and looked at it. The more I looked at it, the more I thought it was a stupid picture.

I tried hard to think that Len would like it, but the longer we were in the line, the more I was sure everyone would think it was silly. I just about ripped it up, but I thought about Len, and I thought he wouldn't think it was stupid, so I didn't.

When it was finally our turn in the line, my mother said to Mrs. Wright, "Tommy insisted on coming to see you."

I held out the paper I had drawn.

"Is this for me?" Mrs. Wright asked.

I nodded. She knelt down and pulled me up close to her. "Tell me about it," she said. Her words reminded me of that day months before when Len had brought my bike back from the auction and I had brought out my treasure box.

I pointed at the picture. "This," I said, "is my lamb, Nosey, that he helped me save."

"He helped you save your lamb?" she asked.

"Twice," I told her. "This," I continued, "is my bike that he bought at the auction and brought to me."

She smiled, and I realized she probably knew about that.

"And what is this?" she asked pointing at another part of my picture.

"That is me and Mr. Wright shaking hands," I said.

"And what do these words down here say?" she asked.

"Friends forever," I answered.

Mrs. Wright threw her arms around me and cried softly. "That is the nicest thing you could have given me," she said. After she hugged me, she looked at me. "I'm sure he will always consider you his friend forever."

19

Where's Tippy?

When Monday came, since I knew that Brian was gone and wasn't coming back, I felt all alone. With both Brian and Len gone, I really hurt inside. I went out and played by myself at recess. Rodney's gang was there again. I tried to avoid them, but Rodney, as usual, had to knock me down.

It was a long week. I was happy when Friday came and I knew the weekend was close. It was also nice because Rodney wasn't at school. His gang still called me names, but they didn't shove me around.

As I rode the bus home, I thought of all of the things that Brian and I had talked about. We were going to run away together. He would take his dog, Deer Hunter, and I would take Tippy and Nosey, and we would live in the woods together where we didn't have to worry about anyone. Now I was alone.

As the bus neared our house, I looked out the window for my two friends. Tippy and Nosey almost always came to meet me, but neither one was there.

As I stepped off of the bus, I called for them, but they didn't come. I thought that if there was a time I really needed them, it was then. I went around to the back of the house and called, but still they didn't come. I checked the barn. I checked the haystack. I looked all over, but I couldn't find my friends. It was already getting dark, and I began to get worried.

My dad came home, and I told him I couldn't find Tippy and Nosey. He asked if I had tried to follow their tracks. I hadn't.

Even though it was March, there was still a lot of snow. Most of it had melted, but it had been a hard winter, so the ground still had a thin layer, and I should have been able to see their tracks. Of course, the two them ran all over the place, so knowing which tracks to follow was almost impossible. Dad said he would come out and help me as soon as soon as he could get his clothes changed.

I went out and tried to find fresh tracks. I found one set that headed out into the pasture south of our house. The three of us didn't go that way very often, so I decided to follow them. As I walked along the tracks, I ran into something that made my heart start to pound. There was a snowmobile trail over the top of Tippy's and Nosey's tracks. We didn't own a snowmobile, so that told me someone else had been in our pasture.

The snowmobile tracks ran in zig zags, with Tippy and Nosey's tracks also zig zagging with them. I began to realize that the snowmobile had been chasing them. I ran faster and faster. I didn't follow Tippy's or Nosey's tracks anymore. I just followed the snowmobile track, since it was easier to see.

Then the trail turned and headed back toward the house. I kept running along the track, and I noticed that the snowmobile trails started crisscrossing. I tried to follow as straight ahead as possible. I reached a point where the track made a sharp turn and headed toward our neighbors' house - the house where Rodney lived.

I had been on a snowmobile once with my cousin, and I knew that turn was sharp enough that someone would have had to come nearly to a stop to make

it. I was just about to turn and follow the snowmobile trail again when, as the sun disappeared, I saw what looked like a brown lump against the snow. I ran as fast I could toward it. As I got closer, I could see that something had been dragged along a path, and the path had a trail of blood.

I felt a horrible pain as I feared what I would find. As I ran, I could feel the tears stinging my eyes. As I reached Tippy, he lay there very still.

"Tippy!" I cried. "Tippy!"

I threw my arms around him and tried to pull him up. I felt a quiver, and he slowly raised his head and whimpered. He looked at me, and I could sense in his eyes that he was saying, "I knew you would come."

"I'm here, boy," I said. "It will be okay, Tippy. We'll get you better."

He only laid his head back down with another whimper.

In the next instant, my dad was standing beside me. He kneeled down and turned Tippy a little and, as he did, Tippy winced and whimpered. When Dad turned him, I could see that Tippy was laying in a pool of blood.

"He's been shot," my dad said.

My dad looked across the field, and I could tell he was looking at the snowmobile trail. It didn't take a genius to know what had happened.

"We can get him better, can't we, Dad?" I asked.

"I'm afraid not," he said. "His wound is so bad, and he has lost too much blood. The best thing we can do is to put him out of his misery." Then, standing and putting his hand on my shoulder, he said, "I'll go get the gun."

As Dad left, I buried my head into Tippy's soft fur and sobbed. I didn't care if I was too old to cry. I couldn't help it. I felt as if my whole body was going to come apart. When I finally got some control of myself I sat down in the snow and pulled Tippy's head into my lap. I stroked his head softly, and told him he had been a good friend to me. I thanked him for saving me from Old Bossy.

"I guess we showed her," I said. I said it hoping that it would make me feel better, but it didn't. But Tippy almost seemed to smile.

By now, it was very dark, and I could see a flashlight getting closer, and knew my dad was coming. He was walking slowly. I knew this was not a job he wanted to do. "Tippy, my friend," I said. "I don't want my dad to have to shoot you."

I couldn't stand the thought of his last moment here being shortened by us. Tippy seemed to know what I was saying. He raised his head off of my lap and turned just enough that he could lick my face, as if to say, "I love you." Then he laid his head back down on my lap, let out a small quiver, and lay still.

I threw my arms around him and sobbed again. "I love you, Tippy. I love you."

When my dad arrived, he knelt down and felt Tippy. "He's gone," my dad said. I could sense the relief in his voice, knowing that he wouldn't have to shoot my dog. My dad helped me to my feet. He handed me the flashlight and gently picked Tippy up. "We will find a nice place to bury him," he said.

As we started toward home, another thought jerked at my heart. "Dad!

Nosey!" I yelled. "I forgot about Nosey!"

I swung the flashlight around, frantically calling for him. It was late, and I knew we should have been milking, but Dad didn't even mention it. He knew I needed to find my lamb.

Daniel showed up. "Dad, what's going on?" he asked.

As Dad turned and Daniel saw Tippy, no more needed to be said. "He needs to find his lamb," Dad said.

Daniel nodded. "I'll help him."

He took the flashlight in one hand and my hand in the other. "How did you find Tippy?" he asked.

I told him about the prints and the snowmobile trail.

"Perhaps we better go back and follow some of the other snowmobile trails," he said.

We walked back to where I had left the trail. We started following it back to the cris-cross area. I was beginning to shiver, my tears freezing on my face. I knew we had to find Nosey soon. If we didn't, in this cold, he'd die.

I called as we went. As we followed one of the trails, it swung back toward where Tippy had been lying, and I saw a small movement ahead of us in the beam of the flashlight.

"Nosey!" I yelled, and I ran to him. Daniel ran after me. When I reached Nosey, he lay there very still, except for gasping when he breathed.

Daniel knelt beside me and looked at the situation. We weren't very far from where Tippy had been. "It appears they ran over Nosey with the snow machine," Daniel said. "It looks like Tippy must have been running ahead and turned back to Nosey when they stopped and shot him."

I looked at where Daniel was shining the light as he summed up everything. I had thought that Tippy had been trying to drag himself toward the house after he was shot, but now I could see he had dragged himself straight toward where Nosey had been run over. Even after he had been shot, he had tried to get to his friend.

I reached down to pick up Nosey, but Daniel stopped me. "We've got to be careful," he said. "Even though he's not bleeding, he could have some internal injuries."

I didn't know what he meant, but I trusted him. Daniel took off his coat and laid it on the ground. He carefully picked Nosey up and put him in it. Daniel wrapped it tightly around him. He handed me the flashlight, gently lifted the bundled lamb onto his shoulder, then took my hand, and we started back.

Nosey didn't move much, but he was breathing hard. When we got back to the house, Dad had already wrapped Tippy in an old blanket. He and Daniel tried to visit quietly, but I couldn't help overhearing what they were saying. Nosey was in such a bad way that they thought they should put him out of his pain.

I begged my dad to let me try to get him better.

Dad shook his head. "He is suffering, and chances are he won't get better. He'll just suffer until he dies."

"Please," I said, trying hard not to cry, "you wouldn't shoot me if I was hurt, would you?"

"That's different," my dad said. "He is a lamb, and you are a person."

"But he's my friend!"

My dad looked away. Life is hard on a farm at times. But letting an animal suffer is not the normal way of things.

"All right," my dad said, "but we can't let it go on forever. If he's not better in a few days, we'll have to end it."

"Ok," I said, hopeful that he would get better.

Daniel carried Nosey out to the barn, and Dad carried Tippy. We laid Tippy in the corner of the newborn calf pen until we could bury him the next day. We fixed a stall with straw for Nosey, and Daniel laid him gently in it. Nosey just laid there, not moving.

Daniel unrolled his coat from around Nosey to check him over. "It looks like he has a broken leg, and probably some cracked ribs, but I can't see anything else."

Daniel said he would splint the leg. He asked me if I could get some nice flat sticks and some gauze. "The flatter the sticks, the more comfortable he will be."

I ran to the house and got the gauze out of the first-aid cabinet, and got some of the roof sticks from my Lincoln Log set.

Daniel looked at the roof sticks when I returned. He knew how much I loved my Lincoln Logs. "Are you sure you want to use these?" he asked. "They'll probably get ruined."

"I don't care," I said.

He carefully wrapped Nosey's leg. He tried to get Nosey to stand or move, but Nosey wouldn't.

"You better get him to eat something," Daniel told me, as he headed to milk the cows.

I got Nosey some milk, but he would only turn his head away from me. I was glad to see him move that much, but I knew he needed the milk, too. When the chores were done, Dad came and put his hand on my shoulder. "We might as well go into the house. If he's still alive in the morning, he might have a chance of surviving."

I didn't want to leave him, but I covered him with an old blanket and followed Dad to the house. It was hard to sleep that night. I was so worried about Nosey. I was glad the next morning was Saturday because I didn't think I could face going to school.

As soon as I could, I rushed to the barn to the pen where we had put Nosey. He wasn't there. I panicked. Had he died? Had someone taken him to bury him? I could feel my eyes filling with tears. Just then Daniel walked in.

"Where's Nosey?!" I cried.

Daniel didn't say anything. He just looked around and then pointed. I looked to where he was pointing. Nosey was over by where my dad had laid Tippy. Nosey was laying beside Tippy, with his head on him. "He must have crawled over there in the night," Daniel said.

As my dad walked in and realized what had happened, he said, "I think we better bury Tippy soon. Maybe, then, your lamb will try to get better."

Daniel carried Nosey back to his pen and gently laid him there. He picked up Tippy, and I got a shovel.

"Where are we going to bury him?" he asked.

I chose a place that was near the haystack, but under a tree, where we had spent a lot of time together. Tippy, Nosey, and I had often laid there in the cool shade while I daydreamed.

"I can help you dig after we get chores done," Daniel said.

"No," I said, "I want to do it alone."

I went with Daniel back to the barn to feed Nosey before I started. I could force the nipple into his mouth, but he would just let the milk drizzle out and wouldn't even swallow. I tried to hold his head up so the milk could run down his throat, but he still wouldn't take it.

I finally decided to go back and start digging Tippy's grave. I dug with all of my might. The ground was still frozen, and I had to use the shovel to chisel through it. I slammed the shovel into the ground harder and harder and harder. As I did, the tears came.

I didn't mean for them to; it just happened. A long time went by. At times, someone in the family would come to help, but I always sent them away.

Mom sent out some water. By the time the sun was almost straight overhead, I was finally breaking through the frozen soil into the soft, loose sand below. Mom sent someone to tell me it was time for lunch, but I told them I wasn't hungry. Usually, this would upset Mom, who thought we should all eat together, but she let it go.

I did think I should take time to try to feed Nosey again, though. I went to the barn and got some milk. Nosey was out of his pen again. He had crawled back over to where Tippy had been laying, even though Tippy was no longer there. I tried and tried to get him to eat, but he wouldn't, so I finally went back to digging the grave.

About the time the sun was ready to go down, I finally had the grave finished. My hands were blistered and bleeding, but I couldn't feel them. They were cold and numb, and that was how I felt inside, too.

I told everyone I was ready, and most of the family came out. Daniel helped me set Tippy's body in the grave, and then we shoveled in the dirt. As I shoveled, my eyes blurred so much that I couldn't even see what I was doing. Dad finally pulled me over and held me close, and I cried. I thought Albert would call me a crybaby, but he didn't, and I didn't care anyway.

We set up a stick for a marker and put some rocks around it. As everyone started to leave, I just stood there and looked at the grave. I remembered how we had chased butterflies together and how we had picked flowers and hunted for rocks. I even kind of smiled as I thought about how he and Nosey would chase cars together. Then I remembered how he had risked his life to save me from Old Bossy, and how the three of us had worked together to get each other to safety, and I fell to my knees and sobbed.

My dad picked me up and held me close, "He was a good dog," he said.

"He was more than that," I said. "He was my friend."

20

Rodney's Gang

fter we buried Tippy, I tried for hours to get Nosey to eat, but he still wouldn't. I tried all day Sunday, except when we had to go to church. I didn't want to go to church. I wanted to be home with Nosey, and I didn't want to think about God anyway. How could He let Tippy die, and why wasn't He helping Nosey get better? But my parents made me go.

It was obvious that Rodney had been the one on the snow machine. His family was one of the few that owned one, the tracks came from his house, and Rodney hadn't been in school. My dad called and talked to his father, but it was clear that Rodney wasn't going to get in trouble. He was an only child, and his parents thought he could never do anything wrong. I knew I wouldn't likely see him at church, because he didn't come very often. But as Sunday evening came, I felt angrier and angrier, knowing I had to go back to school the next day.

My dad must have been able to tell something was wrong, because he asked me what the matter was. I told him that the next time I saw Rodney, he was going to get it.

My dad took me on his lap, and very firmly told me that fighting would help nothing. He would not let me down until I promised I would not fight.

Monday came, and still Nosey wouldn't eat. And no matter how many times we put him in his pen, the next time we came out, he was lying where we had laid Tippy. He would hardly move for us, or show any sign of life, but after we left, he somehow got himself over there.

I finally had to go to school. I wished I was not in the same classroom as Marco. I thought if I could avoid him, Rodney, and their group, I could probably keep my promise to Dad. But recess made it impossible. I tried to avoid them, I truly did, but Rodney and his gang came looking for me.

"So your wittle doggie got shot," Rodney said, mocking me loudly in a baby voice so that everyone near turned to stare.

I didn't answer him.

"Oh, how sad," Rodney continued. "Don't you think that's sad, boys?"

They all agreed with him, nodding and grinning.

Rodney mocked me further, giving me a shove. "And I hear your fluffy little lamb got run over and has a broken leg and is dying." Then he turned to the rest of his gang. "Isn't that sad, boys?"

Again they all nodded, grinning. I couldn't take any more. I turned my back to him and started to walk away.

"Miss Markley laughed when we told her." Rodney taunted, so that I stopped. "Everyone knows they were just stupid animals, almost as stupid as you. They were only good for me to use for target practice."

Suddenly, something happened. I'm not sure what it was, but I felt a feeling inside of me that felt like an explosion. I spun so fast that Rodney was caught by surprise, still grinning, when I hit him square in the face so hard that he hit the side of the school before his feet even touched the ground. He just smashed into the wall and slid down on his back.

Instantly, two of his gang grabbed me. As one tried to hold one of my arms, I brought my fist forward and slammed my elbow back into his stomach with such force it doubled him over. I then spun and, with my other fist, I smashed him so hard in the face that he landed on his back in the mud.

The other one had gone for one of my legs. I brought my fist up and, with all of my strength, I hit him so hard in the side of the face that it knocked him into the dirt, and he let go.

I turned to face Rodney again as he was scrambling to his feet. I hit him again, and again he went down. The last two boys jumped in. They had no sooner touched me than I hit one, knocking him down, and I slammed the other one into the side of the school. The days of hauling hay had made me strong, and I had never felt a feeling like I felt now.

Rodney turned to run and had barely made it to his feet when I tackled him, taking him to the ground. He threw up his arms to protect his face as I hit him again and again. I couldn't stop myself now. The weeks of anger, being pushed around, and being called names, had built up, and it all seemed to come out at once.

Rodney's friends would attack me again and again, and each time, I would knock them to the ground or slam them into the wall, only to turn back to Rodney.

I could think of nothing else, and I didn't even realize everyone had gathered around us, nor did I realize I was bleeding from cuts on my face and from my nose. Soon, Rodney's friends, bleeding and dazed, quit trying to help him. Rodney was taking my whole attack when, suddenly, I felt a strong hand grab my arm.

As I whirled around, ready to hit whoever it was, Miss Markley pulled me around to face her, "Stop it!" she screamed. "You stop it, I say!"

As everyone gathered around us and she held my arm tight, she asked, "What happened here?"

"He started it," one of Rodney's gang said. "He hit Rodney for no reason."

Although some others, including Suzanne, tried to speak, Miss Markley brushed them off. She had heard enough. She had heard what she wanted to believe. She dragged me by the arm into her classroom. She stood me in front of the mirror and said, "Look at yourself!"

I looked. I saw my pants were torn and my shirt hung in pieces. My nose was bleeding, I had cuts all over my face, and both eyes were black. I hadn't known until then that, other than Rodney, I had probably come out the worst. I hadn't even realized I had been hit at all.

"Do you know what we do with little boys that fight?" she asked.

I didn't answer her. As I looked at her, all I could think of was Rodney saying, "Miss Markley laughed". Suddenly I blurted out, "I hate you!"

Miss Markley grabbed the paddle and slammed me down over the desk. As she brought her hand back, I saw in the mirror another hand jerk the paddle from Miss Markley's hand. Miss Markley spun around to face old Mrs. Sange, a woman half her size.

"Give me that!" Miss Markley sputtered angrily.

"What are you doing?" Mrs. Sange asked quietly.

"I am teaching this boy not to fight!" Miss Markley said.

"You are teaching one boy not to take on five boys, all older than him?" Mrs. Sange asked, making it sound like a stupid question.

"Well, they said he started it," Miss Markley said, stumbling over her words.

"Right! He started a fight against all of them!" Mrs. Sange said in disbelief. "And what did he have to say about it?"

"He didn't say anything," Miss Markley said, now much quieter.

"Did you ask him?" Mrs. Sange asked.

"Well, no," Miss Markley stammered.

"Perhaps we should hear his side, don't you think?"

Miss Markley nodded. Mrs. Sange knelt down beside me. "Tommy," she asked, "did you hit Rodney first?"

I nodded. Mrs. Sange looked a little surprised. "Why would you do such a thing?" Mrs. Sange continued. "There are five of them, and they are older than you."

"Because he said he thinks it's funny that he shot my dog and ran over my lamb with his snow machine," I blurted out. I started crying again. I pointed at Miss Markley. "He said she thinks it's funny because they are dumb animals, almost as dumb as me." Then, turning to Miss Markley, I said, "You're just like Rodney! You would have killed them, too! You can beat me, if you want! You can kill me! I don't care, because they were the only friends I had, and I hate you! I hate you! I hate you!"

I flopped down on the desk and sobbed. I just couldn't help it. I expected Miss Markley to jerk the paddle away from Mrs. Sange and start hitting me, but I didn't care. Nothing happened, and I finally looked up. Miss Markley had a strange look on her face, one I had never seen before. Mrs. Sange stood, quietly slipped the paddle back into Miss Markley's hand, and then looked her in the face. Miss Markley looked at the paddle for an instant, then threw it to the floor and ran from the room crying.

Mrs. Sange knelt down beside me again, and put her arms around me, and she, also, cried. When she finished, she pulled out a handkerchief and wiped her eyes, and mine, too. She then stood and took my hand. "Come on. Let's get you cleaned up."

She took me down to the teacher's lounge. No student ever went into the teacher's lounge. We all thought it was a place of great mystery, where teachers planned terrible ways to make kids behave. Some of the older kids even said they had whips, chains, and other things in there. But it was just a simple room with a counter, a fridge, a sink, a table and chairs, and a couch. Mrs. Sange washed my face and bandaged my cuts.

The principal appeared at the door. "What happened?" he asked.

"I think we need to talk later," Mrs. Sange answered quietly.

"But some of the other boy's moms are here to take them home, and they want an explanation now!"

"Then tell them that all five of those boys were picking on one younger boy, and he decided to stand up for himself," Mrs. Sange said.

"And what's the matter with Wanda?" the principal asked. "She just ran out of the school, crying, and she got into her car and left."

"She has some issues to sort through," Mrs. Sange said.

"Who's going to cover her class?"

"Maybe you can," Mrs. Sange answered.

The principal shook his head and walked out.

My mother was called, and I sat in the office to wait for her. When she arrived and saw me, she gasped. She ran to me. "Tommy, what happened?"

I didn't even answer. I just looked down. I didn't feel like talking, and I knew Dad would be mad at me for not keeping my promise.

"I'll go get Mrs. Sange," the secretary said, and she slipped out of the office.

"Tommy, did this have to do with Rodney and Tippy?" Mom asked.

I didn't answer.

She continued. "You know what your father told you. You promised not to fight."

I still didn't answer. I was sure I was going to get punished, and I didn't care anymore. I just wished I could run away. As Mom started to say something again, Mrs. Sange arrived. She invited Mom into the principal's office, and I was left alone. They were in there for a long time.

When Mom came out of the office, she looked at me and said, "Let's go home."

It was a long ride home. Mom kept trying to get me to tell her more about what happened, but I didn't want to talk about it. My face was swollen, and it hurt to move my mouth. We hadn't even come to a complete stop when I jumped from the car and ran for the barn, with Mom calling after me.

I just wanted to get away from there and away from everything, especially away from Rodney's words that kept ringing in my ears. "They were only good for target practice." I ran to the barn to Nosey's pen. He wasn't there. I turned, and he was again lying where Tippy had been. I went and threw my arms around him.

He was still breathing, but his breathing was raspy and shallow. Mom came running in behind me, and stood there for a minute. She knelt down beside me.

"Mrs. Sange told me what happened," she said. "Although I can't say I approve of you fighting, I don't feel I can blame you."

I didn't answer her, so she continued. "I didn't realize how hard of a time you were having at school. I didn't realize the others made fun of you because you couldn't read and write. Mrs. Sange sent this home," she said, holding up a book. "She thought you might like to read it."

I recognized it at once as the book Brian and I would get out of the class library, the one with pictures of trees, mountains, rivers, streams, and lots of animals – the one whose story Brian and I wanted to know.

"Will you read it to me?" I asked.

"No," she answered, "but I will help you learn to read it for yourself."

We sat there quietly for a moment, and then she said, "Lunch will be ready when you want it."

She got up and went into the house. She didn't even scold me about my school clothes that were dirty and torn, nor did she say I needed to go in and change. They weren't worth changing now anyway.

I got some milk and tried to feed Nosey. He wouldn't eat. "Nosey!" I cried, "Nosey, please! Why won't you eat?" I buried my head in his woolly side and sobbed. I was mad at God for taking my dog and causing this all to happen, but at that moment, I didn't know what else to do or who else to turn to, and I needed someone to listen to me. I started sobbing, "Please, God, don't take Nosey. I need him! I need him! Please! Please!"

The tears poured down my face and stung my cuts, but that didn't hurt nearly as bad as my insides did. I didn't think I could live if I lost Nosey, too.

"Please Nosey," I cried as I hugged him. "I need you! I need you!"

I knelt there sobbing, feeling like my heart was going to break, when I felt a small movement in my arms. As I lifted my head, Nosey weakly lifted his and licked my face.

21

Summer Again

fter Nosey licked my
face, I didn't leave his side all
afternoon. When the others got home
from school, Mom sent a sandwich out
to me so I could stay with him. I gave
him a drink whenever I could get him to take one. By afternoon, he had eaten a
small amount of the milk from the bottle. At milking time, my dad came out to the
barn. I was sure I was going to be in trouble for breaking my promise, but he
never mentioned it.

He looked down at Nosey and me and said, "Tommy, don't you think it is
about time we end your little lamb's suffering?"

I held up the bottle and showed him how much Nosey had drunk. "Ok,"
my dad said, "we'll keep trying."

The next day, Nosey drank almost a full bottle. Mom didn't make me go
to school for the rest of the week, but she did have me spend lots of time learning
to read. In between each reading lesson, I ran to the barn to check on Nosey. He
was growing stronger all the time. When I came out Thursday morning, he was
wobbling on his feet, and I got excited. When I gave him his bottle, he didn't
drink it very fast, but he did finish the whole thing. I made sure he had some grain
and hay and anything he would eat.

By the end of the week, Nosey was walking around, and I was reading. I
couldn't believe how easy reading was. I'm not sure why I couldn't get it before.
It was still hard to sound the words out, but I had learned all of the letters and their
sounds. I could figure out most of the words in the books Mom had me try to
read, if I took my time. I guess I had been learning some at school, even though I
thought I hadn't.

On Sunday, Mom decided it was time for me to see if I could read the
book she had brought home. It took me a long time, and I still had to have some
help with the bigger words, but I was able to read it. It was the story of a little
bear and his trip through the woods and the animals he met. I read it again and

again until my brothers asked, then insisted, that I stop.

I got so excited about reading I could hardly take time out for anything else besides feeding Nosey. I even took books out and read them to him.

On Monday, I begged to be able to stay home again. Mom said I could stay home one more day, but she said I had to go back on Tuesday.

"I know you don't want to go back," she said. "But sooner or later, you have to face your problems, and the longer it is, the harder it will be."

Tuesday came. My eyes were still black and my cuts were far from being healed. Dad never punished me for the fight, but before I went back to school, he had a strong talk with me.

"I can't blame you for fighting," he told me. "But I don't want you to make a habit of trying to solve your problems that way."

I told him I had tried not to fight. I had even tried to stay away from Rodney and his gang, but when Rodney said what he did, something happened and I couldn't help myself. Dad told me that a person needs to be in control of his feelings at all times. He talked to me a long time about many other things, most of which I didn't understand, but I trusted my dad, and I promised to avoid fighting.

Normally I would ride the bus, but Dad took me to school this time. I was late, and school had started. Dad didn't even come in with me like I hoped he would. He always says we need to learn to stand on our own.

As I opened the door to my classroom and went in, everyone turned to stare at me. I wanted to turn around and run, but Mrs. Sange said, "Tommy, we're glad to have you back. Why don't you take your seat?"

As I sat down, Suzanne leaned over and whispered, "Rodney got suspended for two weeks. It actually doesn't matter anyway because he's too embarrassed to come to school and show his face."

"My face doesn't look all that good either," I said.

"Maybe," she replied, "but I saw him before his mother came to get him, and yours isn't as bad as his. Besides, there were five of them, and only one of you."

When it came time for the reading groups, Mrs. Sange called for group four. As I started up the aisle, I heard Marco snicker. I turned and looked at him. He still had a black eye and a few cuts of his own. He grinned and mouthed the words, "the stupid group."

We sat down on the chairs, and Mrs. Sange said, "Everyone turn to page one." Then she looked at me and said, "All right, Tommy, let's start with you."

I was shaking. I was wondering if the words would make sense like they did at home, or would they just look like marks on a page like they had before. I looked at the page, and my heart pounded. "The fat cat sat on the hat on the mat," I read.

Instantly it was very quiet in the classroom, and everyone was staring at me. I felt very uncomfortable. Mrs. Sange let out a slight gasp. "Let's turn to page thirty-seven," Mrs. Sange said. I still couldn't read my numbers, so someone had to help me. I could again hear the snickering. "Okay," Mrs. Sange said, "Tommy, read."

A little bit unsure, I sounded out the letters as I read, "When Sam and Ann went to the pond they saw a fox and a duck."

Everyone started talking at once, and I wished I could just hide.

"Well," Mrs. Sange said, "Tommy, I don't see any reason for you to stay in this group. You can go get a book from the class library and read. I want you to come up with group two tomorrow."

As I passed Marco's desk, he glanced away. I went to the class library in the back of the room to choose a book. For the first time, I could read the titles. I chose one that sounded good and went to my desk. As I sat down, Suzanne smiled and whispered, "Good job!"

Mrs. Sange called up group three. Marco got up, glanced at me, and then turned away. I found myself almost saying to him, "The next stupidest group," but I didn't. I looked at him as well as the others going up. They had feelings, just like I did. How could I think about saying something mean when I hated it so much?

When it came Marco's turn to read and he struggled to get the words, instead of hating him, I felt sorry for him. I knew how he felt. Last year, he must have gone through some of what I had gone through this year. Why else would he have been held back? Perhaps the way he acted was just a cover for how he truly felt.

Group three finished just in time for recess. On the way out to recess, everyone wanted to talk to me about what had happened. I found out that the other four boys were suspended for a day each and told they couldn't play together at recess anymore. One girl told me that some of the boys' parents were angry, and went to the principal wanting to have me expelled. Suzanne said that the principal had talked to her and lots of other students. She said almost all of them told about what Rodney and his gang had been doing. After the principal heard everything, it was Rodney's gang that got in trouble.

During the week I was home, I had overheard my dad telling my mom that

Rodney's dad, who had called at first and was very angry, was quick to call back and apologize when he found out the whole story. Dad said, "Mr. Olsen is afraid the school might take further action against Rodney if we press them, and he asked us not to."

I heard my parents talking more, and Dad said, "It will do no one any good to drag this out, especially Tommy. We need to forget it and go on with life."

I'm not quite sure what he meant by "go on with life." At first I was scared, thinking he meant someone might die. I knew I didn't actually mean to hurt anyone. But when I asked him, he said he just meant we need to forget what had happened. I think it will be hard to forget.

I do know I would be happy to forget it, especially at recess. I was nervous about what that would be like. As I walked outside, most of the students from the school gathered around me. "I can't believe you whipped them all!" someone said. "You sure showed them!" another person added. "They don't pick on anyone anymore!" a boy said, patting me on the back. A girl nodded. "It was about time someone stood up to them and made them leave us alone."

I was embarrassed. Everyone acted like I was a hero for something I hadn't wanted to do, and I didn't like all of the attention.

Kathleen grabbed my arm. "We could use somebody else to play tag."

Then I saw Suzanne holding the kickball. "Would you like to come play kickball with us?" she asked.

I turned toward Suzanne. "But I've never played kickball before."

"That's okay," she answered. "Everyone has agreed you can be a captain."

Everyone nodded. Steve was the other captain. We started choosing sides. I chose Suzanne first. I didn't even know if she could play, but she was the nicest, and besides, I didn't even know if I could play. Steve chose Jason. I chose Tim. Steve chose Lori. I was just ready to make my next choice when I saw Marco behind the back stop.

Suzanne saw me glance over at him. "Now that Rodney's gang can't play together, he has no one to be friends with," she whispered.

"David," I called as my next choice.

"Sally," Steve said.

I could see Marco hanging his head. I could tell he wanted to be chosen. But he had been one of Rodney's gang. The week before he had been one of the ones punching me, telling me Tippy and Nosey were stupid. I felt angry.

"Jack," I said.

"Fred," Steve said.

I looked at Marco again. I remembered the times I would hang around the back stop, hoping someone would choose me, acting like I wasn't there to be chosen, so I wouldn't be disappointed when I wasn't. Suzanne touched my arm, and as I looked at her, she nodded her head toward Marco. She seemed to understand how I felt and still wanted me to call him.

But he had laughed when Rodney said that all Tippy and Nosey were good for was target practice. I felt angry again, and I was just about to call for Bill, when I thought about Suzanne's words, "He has no one to be friends with." Rodney's gang had been mean to Suzanne, too, but here she was trying to get me to choose Marco.

"Tommy," Steve said, "it's your turn."

I bit my lip and swallowed hard. "Marco," I called out. Suzanne smiled at me, and her smile alone would have been pay enough, but when Marco lifted his head, I could see a brightness in his eyes and his smile. It was the biggest smile I had ever seen.

There was a little commotion. I couldn't tell if my team agreed or not, but I could tell they were shocked. Both teams were. I was. Marco was. I think he thought there was a chance Steve might call him, but not me. Steve was so surprised he forgot to call someone else.

"It's your turn, Steve," I said.

I'm not sure who won the game. Both teams felt they had the most points, but no one kept score. I was so happy to get to play kickball for the first time, and I found out I wasn't too bad. Most of my team acted nervous about Marco at first, but Marco's excitement rubbed off on everyone. He pounded each team member on the back after each play, even if they didn't do very well.

Suzanne said, "This is Marco's first time getting to play kickball, too."

I could hardly believe that was true. "But with kindergarten, he has been here for two years before this one."

Suzanne nodded. "That's true. But no one has ever picked him. Last year they called him 'dummy' because he couldn't read and had been held back a year."

I didn't understand. Why would someone do to another person what they hated so much themselves? I don't think I will ever understand.

At lunch recess, I got to be team captain again. After what happened in the morning, I decided to choose people first that were chosen last the time before, at least after I chose Suzanne. Steve was the other captain again, and he seemed to want to also. We included everyone from Rodney's gang on the two teams; everyone, that is, except Rodney. He hadn't come back to school yet.

It was more than two weeks after I returned to school that Rodney finally came back. The first time I saw him, he just turned away, but not before I noticed both of his eyes were still slightly black, and his cuts hadn't quite healed. I hadn't realized how mean I had been.

When he came hanging around the back stop where we played kickball, I just couldn't get myself to choose him for my team, no matter how hard I tried. Suzanne even tried to get me to, but I just couldn't. I couldn't get the image of him shooting Tippy out of my mind.

Rodney began to hang around with older kids, kids who did things everyone said were wrong. One day, Rodney didn't come to school. Everyone whispered that he was in the hospital. He had taken something that made him very sick.

I felt bad. I realized that even Rodney needed to have some friends. In church that Sunday, we talked about doing something for him. Our teacher had a card that we all signed. We took it and some homemade cookies to him later that week. He was home by then, but he still looked sick. He was happy to see us.

I was getting more and more excited about school every day. I loved to read, and I read everything I could get hold of. Mrs. Hillard came back, and Mrs. Sange left, and I missed her. But Mrs. Hillard let me keep a book at my desk just like Mrs. Sange did. I learned numbers, and I did my work fast so I could read. I passed everyone except Lori on how many books they had read for the year, and I was getting close to her number. I read lots, hoping to pass her by the end of school.

I was moved up to reading group one only a few days after I had been moved to group two. Marco even moved up a group. We weren't really friends, but if I was assigned to work with him, I didn't mind. He started being nice to me.

Everyone began to forget about the fight because Rodney's gang was gone. I became just me again, which I liked much better.

We started working on a special end of year project. We got to choose what we would do, and I knew exactly what mine would be. I spent every free minute I could on it, and I couldn't wait to show it to Nosey.

Nosey was still getting better. He hadn't ever become his old, chipper self though. He never chased cars anymore. It probably didn't seem the same to him without Tippy.

He started putting some weight on the leg he had broken, and as the snow was almost all melted, I would take him outside for a short time. That seemed to cheer him up. I liked it, too, especially when I would get off of the bus from school and I could hear the geese honking overhead as they headed north. That meant summer was coming.

One day, I got off of the bus, and there was a meadowlark sitting on a post right by our mailbox singing his song. I knew that the pastures would soon be all melted, and the buttercups would be blooming again. I was finding it harder and harder to concentrate in school.

Then, on one of the last days of school, the sun was shining down nice and warm as I got off of the bus. I decided I would take Nosey for a walk out through the sagebrush. By then, the cows were already out to pasture, and their milk tasted of the wild onions that grow in the spring.

I changed and went out to see Nosey like I always did. He wasn't there. I was really scared. I ran all through the barn calling him, but I couldn't find him anywhere. I ran out the door, into the pasture, everywhere I could think of, but I couldn't find him. I was running to the house to  call Dad when I heard a "baa." I turned toward the old tree, and there was Nosey. He was lying on Tippy's grave.

"Would you like to take a walk in the pasture?" I asked him. He just raised his head and looked at me, then laid his head back down. I don't know if he knew it was Tippy's grave or not. I don't know how he could. I hadn't ever taken him there. Before Tippy died, the three of us would sit there in the shade a lot. But there seemed to be more to it than that.

I got him to follow me to the pasture, and he even romped a little, but the minute we got back, he went over to the old tree, and quietly laid down on Tippy's grave again. Nosey was way too big for me to carry, so I couldn't drag him back to the barn. I couldn't get him to leave Tippy's grave until he had been there for a while, even if I offered him grain.

Every day from then on, when I got off of the bus, Nosey would be lying on Tippy's grave. No matter how well I locked him in the barn, he would be there.

Finally, it was the last day of school. It was only a half day, so the sun was still high overhead when I got home. I hurried and tossed my things in the house and ran outside. Sure enough, Nosey was lying on Tippy's grave again.

"Look what I've got," I said to him. "It's a story I wrote. Do you want to hear it?"

He raised his head, looked at me, and baaed as if to say yes.

"Let's go pick some flowers for Tippy first," I said.

He got up and followed me into the pasture. The afternoon sun was warm as we walked the path we had walked so many times. Only this time there were only two of us instead of three. We found a beautiful meadow full of bright yellow flowers. They looked like a carpet of sunshine. We picked a nice bunch and arranged them with a few pieces of sagebrush and wild onions. We then went back and carefully laid them on Tippy's grave.

Nosey laid down on the grave, and I sat down beside him with my back to the tree. I opened the book, the project I had worked on so hard the last few months of school. I had drawn pictures and everything. Nosey raised his head and laid it in my lap. I stroked the soft wool on his neck as I began to read.

"Once there was a little boy named Tommy, who was also known as Super Cowboy. He had a dog named Tippy and a lamb named Nosey. They loved to play together in the pasture, on the haystack, or just do nothing at all. You see, they were all best friends..."

If you enjoyed our book, we would love to have you do a review on Amazon at:

http://amzn.com/1629860026

ACKNOWLEDGEMENTS

A big thanks to all of those who have helped me edit this book, especially to my wife, Donna, for all of her help editing and encouragement in writing.

IMAGES ACKNOWLEDGEMENTS

- Can Stock Photo Inc. / ebphoto: canstockphoto.com
- Byron Bates
- Shutterstock: shutterstock.com
- Brian Raty
- Yassine
- Cover: Mark McKenna

Read other stories, purchase more books, or sign up for a short story each week by going to
http://www.publishinginspiration.com

Other books
by
Daris Howard

Daris Howard Amazon page: http://amzn.com/e/B004H76UGK

Life's Outtakes books
(52 humorous and inspirational Stories in each book)

When The World Goes Crazy - Life's Outtakes Year 1

All's Well Here - Life's Outtakes Year 2

When Life Is More Than We Dreamed - Life's Outtakes Year 3

Nothing But A Miracle - Life's Outtakes Year 4

Singing To The End Of Life - Life's Outtakes Year 5

It's Ninety Percent Mental - Life's Outtakes Year 6

Angels Among Us - Life's Outtakes Year 7

Other Books

***Under Open Skies* - Born To Run, Live To Be Free**
http://amzn.com/1629860042
In this second book in the *Under Open Skies* series, Tom Johnson is now 25 years old and married. Going to school and trying to take care of his family, he gets a job taking care of horses. When the lady he works for purchases an old, former race horse, and Tom needs to take care of him, Tom learns the true meaning of freedom.

The Three Gifts - http://amzn.com/1449961436
A beautiful Christmas story about three young men who are convicted of mugging little children for their Halloween candy. Instead of sentencing them to jail, as is expected, the judge sentences them to 100 hours of community service babysitting at the Women's Crisis Center.
They were prepared for jail, but they were not prepared for what was in store for them as the children opened their eyes and hearts and changed their lives.

The Mail-Order Bride - http://amzn.com/1480200387

It was to be the big day for Eli. His fiancé, Molly, was coming in on a ship. Two years earlier, unable to find work in England, he had headed for America. His ship was caught in a storm, and he ended up, not in Pennsylvania as he planned, but in Newfoundland.

But that was all behind him now. He had written to Molly every day for the two years, and now she was coming so they could be married.

But Eli was in for a surprise. Unknown to him, Molly had married. She had bought him a mail-order bride, and Eli's life was going to suddenly take an unexpected twist.

Essence Of The Heart, The Royal Tutor -
http://amzn.com/1479392189

Mystery, Intrigue, And Clean Romance!

When he is called before the queen, Jacob, the handsome, young Captain of the Royal Guard, is sure it is to discuss the baffling increase in assassination attempts against the royal family. Instead, the queen assigns the shocked young captain to tutor her out-of-control, tomboy daughter, Marie.

He knows all of the other tutors have failed miserably, and he tries to beg out of it, but the queen will not relent. However, she does give him leave to use any teaching method he likes. Her ultimate command is that she be trained as a lady in preparation for her royal ball.

Angry and humiliated at what he feels is a degrading and impossible assignment, especially for a military captain, he determines to train the princess like he would one of his guardsmen. He will demand strong discipline, tough academics, and sword combat training. He is sure that his rigorous approach will push the princess to complain to her mother, who will then remove him from the assignment.

But to his surprise, Marie instead responds positively to the harsh discipline, and becomes a princess like no other.

And, when they come under attack, her training might be just enough to save both of their lives as they work to unravel who is behind the assassination attempts, and also try to solve the mystery of why the Lord High Chamberlain is such a great sword fighter.

About The Author

Daris Howard is an author and playwright who grew up on a farm in rural Idaho. He associated with many colorful characters including cowboys, farmers, lumberjacks and others. Besides his work on the farm he has worked as a cowboy and a mechanic. He was a state champion athlete and competed in college athletics. He also lived for eighteen months in New York.

Daris and his wife, Donna, have ten children and were foster parents for several years. He has also worked in scouting and cub scouts, at one time having 18 boys in his scout troop.

His plays, musicals, and books build on the characters of those he has associated with, along with his many experiences, to bring his work to life.

Daris is a math professor and his classes are well known for the stories he tells to liven up discussion and to help bring across the points he is trying to teach. His scripts and books are much like his stories, full of humor and inspiration.

He and his family have enjoyed running a summer community theatre where he gets a chance to premiere his theatrical works and rework them to make them better. His published plays and books can be seen at http://www.darishoward.com. He has plays translated into German and French and his work has been done in many countries around the world.

In the last few years, Daris has started writing books and short stories. He writes a popular news column called *Life's Outtakes*, which consists of weekly short stories and is published in various newspapers and magazines in the U.S. and Canada including **Country**, **Horizons**, and **Family Living**.